LITTLE SISTERS OF THE APOCALYPSE

LITTLE SISTERS
OF THE APOCALYPSE

KIT REED

BLACK ICE
BOOKS

Copyright © by Kit Reed
All rights reserved
First edition
First printing 1994

Published by Fiction Collective Two with support given by
the English Department Publications Unit of Illinois State
University, the English Department Publications Center of
the University of Colorado at Boulder, the Illinois Arts
Council, and the National Endowment for the Arts.

Address all inquiries to: Fiction Collective Two, c/o English
Department, Publications Center, Campus Box 494, University of Colorado at Boulder, Boulder, CO 80309-0494

Little Sisters of the Apocalypse
Kit Reed

ISBN: Paper, 0-932511-95-3

Produced and printed in the United States of America
Distributed by the Talman Company

For Katy Reed, woman extraordinaire,
who gave the title, which supplied the story

1

Context: In bad times writers have resources. K. attends her mother, who is dying. The first thing to die is the will. The second will be the intellect. The body will take longer. Her daughter turns to narrative. The object? Name a place. People it. Go there.

Drawn back and back again to the parched lakefront that surrounds the women's colony, Chag paces her balcony like a widow's walk, stalking without knowing why she is so restless. There is a difference today, a shift in the light or a faint disturbance in the air, the stir of impending change. It brings her to the rail with her arms spread, leaning out like a brilliant figurehead, classic: woman, staring out to sea. What's out there? What?

What is it?

"Toby?"

Nothing moves on the bleached lakebed and there is nothing in the sky but the unremitting sun. Nothing. But there is a change in the air today, a hum or vibration that suggests something is coming. The men, on their way back into the territory? The army returning? Chag does not know.

The prospect leaves her both joyful and frightened.

Without them the island is so peaceful!

The men are all gone, at least all the men the women care about. They are off at some war. It is the ultimate sexist act. Understand, the women of Schell Isle are alone here because the men are away at the last great adventure, *the one place you can't go*. Still Chag is distracted, caught—short—by intimations. There is something going on out there.

❖

HUDN HUDN. RMMM RMMM. RMMMMMMM. In an underground garage a world away from here the air vibrates with the rumble of motors.

❖

"It's getting weird out. We need to beef up the armaments."

Courtney Ravenal comes in at least once a week with this. Chag's beautiful, bellicose second-in-command is intent on arming the battlements, preparing to repel all boarders.

Chag sighs. "Now what is it?"

Courtney hisses, "They could come back any time."

She and Courtney tug back and forth over everything— principles, issues, the laws of this strange city. The unidentifiable but palpable change in the atmosphere—the disturbance in the air—has left Chag trembling at the possibilities. Stirred, expectant, she studies her second in command and decides to tell her nothing. Chag says carefully, "What makes you think so?"

"Something I found," she says angrily, "Some kind of warning."

Chag says, "What are you afraid of?"

Courtney taps the Colt she wears strapped to her thigh. "You know. The Return." She twists her scarf as if it's her lover's neck she is wringing. "Shit! They try to come back, we blow them out of the water."

Toby. "No! We love them."

"Speak for yourself, bitch."

"Then they love us," Chag says, shaken.

"What makes you so sure?" Courtney produces an object so alien that Chag feels doubts like licking flames in her belly. "Look at this!" It is a fetish: hair, glass shards and gems wired to bone in an odd pattern.

Chag knows better than to tell Courtney that she too has something unusual to report. She dissembles. "Could be anything." It could. Courtney's always coming in with invented crises, angry and desperate for action.

"It's a fucking warning. I say we arm. Blow them out of the water." This is an unintended irony. The lake dried up years ago.

"Stop," Chag says. "Relax. It's nothing."

"You want to lie down and roll over for them?"

Chag is perhaps too firm. "I said, it's nothing. You don't even know what you're afraid of," she says, dismissing her. This is a lie. She does know what Courtney is afraid of. Courtney's afraid of the same thing Chag's afraid of.

The fault line in her heart. *Toby.* Of course she wants him back. But with him come love and loss, conflict, confusion and disorder. Without him, she is autonomous.

God she misses him.

❖

—But look at this nice safe place I made for you. Departing,

9

he raised the goggles on his leather flier's helmet/ brilliant in his silver suit he lifted the faceplate/ threw his boat cloak over his shoulder/ put his cap on her head and hugged her so hard that her chin hit the gold braid on his shoulderboard. Then he put her in her place. Sweet talk keeps her there.

—You'd be so nice to come home to.

❖

The island is far from the unknown front where the men are fighting. In the ultimate refinement of wartime technology they keep their location secret.

Descended from the first gated communities designed to insulate the prosperous, Schell Isle is still and beautiful. A manmade paradise, it sits like a gem in the middle of an artificial lake. When the men left, the lake was filled. Blue water glistened in a thousand points under the desert sun. In those days heat mirages shimmered above blue waters. Never mind whose territory the men flooded to create this or who they had to displace. Never mind the Outlaw family, exiled to their barrio; nobody cares about the poor. They won't be back; security is superb.

It's as different from the smoke and blood and confusion of the front as life from death. The men say they hate what they're doing but they love it. It assuages their guilt to think of the women they leave behind as safe in beautiful surroundings.

—This place is forever.

The men congratulated themselves and left. As they did, the lake went dry. To the women the receding water was like a reproach. *This is what happens without a man around to take care of things*.

Even though the water is gone the women prefer to live as if it still exists, pining on private docks, listening as the dry breeze whistles in long-dead cattails. Although the lakebed is flat and smooth the women cross the bleached surface by causeway. They say this is because they can't afford car trouble with the men gone; they say it's only prudent, but Chag knows better.

It's the possibilities.

What lies just beneath the sandy crust? Perhaps it's something huge and omnivorous, hunched to break the surface. Enemies may storm the electronic barrier at the perimeter and come swarming down on you or there may be supernatural forces at work: nature poised to avenge the families who used to make their homes here. Broach the lakebed and water may gush forth under the wheels of your BMW like the Red Sea drowning the pharoah's chariots.

This is not really what the women are afraid of.

The women are afraid if they set foot on the dry lakebed they may rouse and summon legions. One misstep and the sky will turn black with the planes of returning men.

About the men.

The women are, at best, ambivalent. *Do we want him back?* Yes.

No. *Look what he has made of us*. Potential widows and orphans. Everything waits on the Return, for which no date has been announced.

"The girl he left behind." Sure. Fixed in place by waiting.

Do we want him back? It is an open question.

It's so peaceful without him. No jealousy, little friction, no

11

yelling. Nobody to come in the door and throw his things down and bypass "How've you been?" to ask without even looking at her, "What's for dinner?"

❖

A breeze lifts dried palm fronds; small creatures scuttle through black shadows and birds plummet, flattening themselves in the white sand, struck down by intimations of some unseen power.

In the sunshot houses and shops of Schell Isle the other women lose track of what they're doing. They stop in the streets, putting down briefcases and shopping bags. Distracted, they lift their heads: *Who called?* Nobody answers.

They're afraid to ask: Do you hear it too? Nobody wants to admit it. *Oh it was just.* Nobody knows just what it was. They shrug and push back their hair and pick up whatever they were doing.

❖

Chag's house is the biggest in the women's colony; her balcony is the highest. If something's out there she will be the first to see it. Something she can neither see nor hear makes her whip her head around. What? There's no sound but the hiss of wind in dried palm fronds and the murmur of the island machinery. The manmade vista never changes.

Still! She says aloud, "Toby?"

Nobody answers but something makes her shiver. Intent, Chag leans out with arms spread, with her eyes wide and her mouth open.

What is it?

12

The glistening sand of the dried lakebed gives back nothing. There's no change in the humming electronic barrier and no activity at the tollgate the women maintain to protect the causeway.

What is it anyway? What is it that stirs Chag and sets her spinning, trying to locate it? What excites the other women for reasons they can't name; what makes them so uneasy? Nothing you can identify. Some subtle change in the tempo or the light? No.

It's nothing Chag can name. Or is it? My God, she thinks and the implications make her belly tremble. Is it them? What if it really is them? What if they're really coming?

❖

It doesn't matter who the women are in real life, right now all they are is waiting. This is what wars make of women: prisoners of waiting. In real life Chag is a poet, but now she's cursed by bitter, inescapable rhymes; they're all that come.

In a flash the runner stumbles;
That's the way the cookie crumbles.

Like the others Chag said goodbye to her life partner, her loving adversary Toby Hagen for, she thought, the good of their country. For once she and her beloved have left off the collision of yang/yin, will and intellect, the lifelong tangle of conflicting egos. She put her arms around his neck and managed not to cry "Don't go," knowing at the same time that war is more important to men than any love affair. What's love, when lives are at stake? Kissed him goodbye and let him go.

And tried not to resent it.

It's been five years. For five years she and the other women

13

have been waiting. Sometimes Chag thinks waiting is all they are. The war is like a foreign country they're barred from entering. Watching the TV nightly news, tapes of blurry frontline coverage beamed in to satisfy them that there's a reason for all this, Chag scans the fuzzy faces like a speed reader, looking for Toby. *Is this all I am?* she thinks. *Just waiting?*

❖

Marking time until it's over.

❖

Walk out on her, put her in place and close the door for five years. Come back and expect to find her where you put her with her arms wide and the place unchanged. Expect her to turn on like the light in the refrigerator when you remember to open it. Shining for you and you only.

❖

Listen to some of the things the men say to you when they go out the door with no set return date and no promises.

"I love you but I have to do this."

Sure.

"I'm doing it for you." Look at him: natty in that uniform, in love with sleek weapons too secret to describe to you. *That's classified.* When he walks out that door he will forget you.

He may give you a present, a token of ownership to mark you, service emblem in gold, class ring in miniature—his

14

thing, scaled down. "Wear this for me."

This is how he leaves in place the apparatus to keep his systems going: "I'm counting on you to take care of things."

See him kiss you the way Toby Hagen kissed Chag when he put her down in this splendid house and said, "Take over for me, OK?"

Chag didn't say: *What if I don't want to?*

Toby didn't say: *Too bad.* He didn't have to. He only said, "I know you'll take good care of things."

Which is what finds Charlotte Hagen in charge here, taking over for Toby. A thwarted poet, she is Acting Governor of Schell Isle. Not governor. The nameplate he had made for her reads Acting Governor. She maintains systems and wrangles over policy with Courtney. Courtney, who goes to extremes, wants Chag to govern with a heavier hand. "Control," she growls, without explaining what she thinks needs controlling. If there isn't trouble, Court will make it.

Therefore Chag must stay ten jumps ahead, anticipating contingencies, making decisions before Courtney can pre-empt them. She's tied to the phone and the computer, doing Toby's job in Toby's absence when all she really she wants is to find the right words for things and set them marching in order. She never wanted this. She'd like to be herself—pure Chag—without complications. She'd like to read Chag's mind when it is empty and uncluttered.

But until or unless he comes back to release her she is this. Custodian. Prisoner. Waiting isn't good for her.

✣

Beware. With responsibility comes power. When he comes back he will find you are different.

Responsibility forges you.

So does independence. Absence. Loss. Do they make you bitter?

Released from the daily imperatives of life with their mates and lovers, released from the responsibility of a paired soul, the women are changing.

From the beginning Chag worried; is Toby all right? Hungry? Hurt? Is he warm enough? Then he was declared missing in action. God, has the war killed him? She'd just like to know one way or the other. She's angry at him for going, scared. She misses him so *much*.

Change your life. Get strong. Run the world without him and you are still hung up his absence.

❖

At the Atlantic Coast Line Terminal in St. Petersburg, Florida, K. and her mother said goodbye to her father, who commanded a submarine. The exercise was not to let him see you cry. Officers' children didn't. She was eight years old.

❖

These are the songs men sing as they stand poised with one foot out the door and the staff car outside with the motor running:

—Keep the home fires burning.

—I love you and I want you to wait for me.

—It's something I have to do.

—I'm doing this for us.

—I'll be back as soon as this thing's over.

—I could not love thee half so much loved I not honor

16

more.

—I won't be back till it's over over there.

—I love you but I have to do this.

Enough, we know what you're in love with.

Men say, Wait here, sit tight, stay pretty for me, when they mean, *We have the power to widow you or orphan you. Present or not, we are in charge here. See how we make you defend our institutions.*

War puts a woman in her place. Give her a man to love—father or son, mate or lover—and you make her vulnerable. Send that man to war and you have domesticated her. Put him in danger and you strip her of her powers. She will guard the hearth and go crazy with worry. In the long run it makes no difference whether the men are captured or torched or even nuked out of existence.

Gone is just as gone.

In some ways, gone is worse than dead.

With dead, at least it's over.

❖

The telegram comes in the middle of the night. The Navy Department regrets to inform you that LTCDR John R. Craig, U.S.N. is missing in action. For the rest of K.'s life he will be missing in action.

❖

Toby is missing in action.

It is this that keeps Chag prisoner on her balcony, looking out as though for a ship that's long overdue and may be lost at sea. Uncertainty. Even if it is the men out there, even if they're coming back, she can't know whether Toby is with them.

Missing is not the same as Killed. Killed is final. They have found the body and tagged it and when this thing is finished he may be mailed back to you for burial. You will get the coffin with the American flag and the bugler will play "Taps" at his funeral. They may send you his sword. Something you can hold in your hands and look at with the knowledge that you are closing this chapter.

Missing is never over. Maybe they made a mistake. War is jumbled, these things happen. When you know where he is, you can think about other things. When you don't know where he is, he is all you think about. Open a letter that comes weeks after he's declared Missing and wonder when he wrote it. Think about him in a prison camp, helpless in some hospital ward with his face blown away along with his fingerprints, think about him barefoot and unarmed in enemy territory, sleeping in shacks and crawling at night, trying to make his way back to you. Think about what he looks like now, after all he's been through and all these years since you last saw him.

Above all, protect his integrity. Put his picture on your desk and keep his clothes fresh and his shoes waiting on the shoe rack he made with that officer's precision and whatever you do, keep everything running just the way he left it. Do all this and recite certain prayers or name the things he loved like so many charms and never, ever let your concentration waver and he just may come back to you.

Do *one thing* wrong and you have lost him.

As long as she can keep things running, everything clicking exactly as Toby did when he was governor, Chag keeps alive the hope that he'll come back to her.

18

❖

The Navy named a ship after K.'s father. Her mother never remarried. Without him she was stripped of her job description: Jack's wife. The loss disenfranchised her.

❖

"Dammit, Chag! Charlotte!"

"What?" A shadow falls like a sword across Chag's balcony. God, she thinks. It's late. How long have I been standing here?

"Something's come up."

"Not again." *Oh, it's you.* "What do you want, Courtney?"

"I tried to warn you. This is big." Days have passed, but Court won't let it go. She stands in front of the setting sun, a negative image haloed in pink light, slapping her automatic angrily. Beautiful as she is, Courtney goes to extremes because she's always angry.

Chag asks, "How do you know?" when what she really wants to ask is, *What makes you so angry?*

"I don't know. I just know I know it. That thing I found. Vibes." She growls, "I think we're in for something bad here." Pale and beautiful with her Snow-White hair, Courtney paces in her tough boots like Nelson or Napoleon. "It's time to get your ass in gear."

"Relax," Chag says. "There's nothing going on here."

It's as if she hasn't spoken. Courtney levels charges: "I suppose you want us to throw it all away."

"What?"

"All this. Everything we've done here. Are you going to just let them walk back in and take it all away from us?"

19

"Who, Court?" She honestly wants to know. "What?"

"If I knew I wouldn't be here." It's too late in the day to be doing this; the dead lake is too quiet and the evening skies are too lovely to turn her back on but Courtney grabs Chag's arm. "We have to act fast. Something big is coming down."

Something big.

Something.

It's in the air. Chag knows it, but that's all she knows.

Courtney is shouting. "Didn't you see that fucking fetish?"

Chag says wearily, "OK, Court. What do you want me do?"

"Not here. I can't talk about it here. Your office."

"OK." Chag leads the way down into the ground floor office and when the door is shut and she's behind her desk with Courtney facing her she sighs. "What?"

"Post extra guards. Arm the perimeter." Courtney's jaw juts; her color is high. She says grimly, "Shoot on sight."

Chag needs to hear her name names. "Who? The Outlaws?"

"Fuck the Outlaws." Raking her black hair with angry fingers Courtney rasps, "They could come back any time."

"You mean the men." Chag's heart lurches. Touching the name plate Toby had made for her she says, "This is their place too."

"Not any more," Courtney says. Her gesture indicates the office; the file cabinets that Chag hates, the winking screens waiting for her to get back to her responsibilities. "You want to give this up? You really want to give this up?" She's getting loud. "You want to give it all back? You want to go back to being nothing?"

She shrugs. "We're supposed to be taking care of things."

Courtney cuts her off. "Forget what we're supposed to be. We're different people now."

"Let's take this one thing at a time," Chag says. Chag, who has a lot of material to process right now.

"You mean give in. Turn back into an accessory."

"It won't be like that." The hell of this is, Chag's not so sure.

"It's going to take all the muscle we have. Guns. Troops."

"Our women aren't... Nobody's that mad at them."

"They will be when the time comes." Courtney smacks the Colt down on the desk. "You want to go back to being what you were?"

Troubled, Chag says in a low voice, "What am I now?"

Courtney chooses not to hear. "You take charge or I will."

Slowly, Chag opens the desk drawer where she keeps the automatic Toby bought her for protection. She doesn't bring it out. She just puts her hand on it. This is how Chag turns her lieutenant aside, Chag, who does not yet know how she feels about the Return or even the possibility of the Return: "First bring me proof."

"Proof!"

"Proof, Court." Chag slams her gun on her desk. "We don't stir people up for no reason."

"Put that away."

Chag taps the gun. "We don't waste our resources on shadows."

"This isn't a shadow," Courtney says. "That fucking fetish."

"For all I know you made it." She bears down. "What have you seen, Court? What have you really seen?"

It's Courtney who's backing off now. "You don't have to see a thing to..."

21

"What have you heard?" Chag presses her hard. "What have you heard about, that you're so afraid of?"

"You don't have to hear a thing to..."

"Don't give me that. What do you know, Court? What do you know really?"

"Nothing yet. I..."

"There." Shit! Q.E.D. "You can't act on nothing. You can't arm the whole island against nothing." Surprised, Chag finds she's holding the gun on her lieutenant. Courtney backs into the doorway with her face fixed in a scowl and her black hair electrified as Chag closes in on her. "Come back when you have something."

"Count on it." Backing out, Courtney slams the door.

❖

Chag sits down at her desk. When she looks up, it is night.

❖

Never mind what the men did to the world to disrupt all but the most rudimentary of communications. The satellites have all been down for decades, the fiberoptic network destroyed, overhead cables severed and the buried ones blasted out of existence. The island's computer system is self-contained; communications are limited to the island Internet.

Suffice it to say the women are essentially cut off here.

This is why Chag's so surprised when her screen flickers and comes to life unbidden. There is a message. It begins, *Tell no one*. It's only a fragment, a transmission begun and hastily interrupted. It could be anything: from the men, a police warning about the Outlaw family. A threat. A caution.

22

Be ready.

Without knowing what, exactly, Chag knows some huge force is moving in their direction. The air shifts, as if making a place for it to rush into.

❖

And in a ruined city so remote from Schell Isle that Chag has never heard its name, sixteen bikers roll out of an underground garage and into the cold morning. Their black helmets are bisected by sleek crosses in silver. Warm breath mists the smoked face plates. The leader raises her gloved hand.

Ready?

The sixteen dip their heads briefly and cross themselves. In ordinary times the bikers dazzle with new software at the top of the Pearson Tower in the blasted city, but today they have business elsewhere. In ordinary times the women are brilliant hackers, who market technology to support their mission to the homeless. They pray together four times a day and when circumstances permit, they meditate. In gentler times they would have been contemplatives.

But in this continuum the savage world demands more. When people are starving you can't just turn your backs and pray for them. Right now life is uncertain and time is short. There's too much to be done here.

The women pursue their God at lightspeed. Brilliant, driven, the bikers devise computer programs in an attempt to address the Almighty. Like divers they are poised for the ultimate leap. Let the computer vault everything that's gone before, leapfrogging millennia of prayer and effort; let the analog mind pursue possibilities at speeds it's impossible to comprehend; let it take them to the new jumping-off point. Then let it begin. For the gifted ones, who come closest to pure contemplation, time spent any other way is a necessary sacrifice. Love-struck and drawn, the women yearn only for the Presence, but even among themselves these bikers will not acknowledge which of them has come close, for fear God may hear them trying to describe what has been given and take it away.

They raise their own vegetables in the city park behind their office block. They celebrate the Sacrament of the Eucharist with the occasional transient priest; they try to do God's will and they try not to resent the male hierarchy that tells them they are only women, and therefore not fit to be His priests.

They pray for the dead and when they have to, they ride out on their bikes to defend the living.

Their legend precedes them: crimes interrupted by the mysterious riders; lives saved at the last minute by bikers roaring to the rescue, robberies thwarted, murderers stopped; children rescued from floods or snatched from under the wheels of runaway cars at the last possible minute; householders saved from foreclosure by an astonishing gift of money; evildoers foiled and the helpless—helped. Picked up from the gutter and handed new lives, the blessed run to the door—too late—in an attempt to say thank you.

Before they can be identified, the mystery riders are on their bikes and gone, whisked away with a roar, disappearing in a cloud of oily exhaust.

Householders stand in the doorway, baffled. Who *was* that...

What do we have to reckon with?

Riding with black scarves streaming, the bikers do not

24

advertise. Surprise gives them the advantage. Mystery makes them powerful; they give their lives to it. Pressed to name the source of their strength, they can only partially explain, although they've spent a lifetime trying to comprehend it.

They are riding out for a reason, and if only the leader knows what it is and she only imperfectly, no matter.

It's enough to know something needs doing.

So it is over the lakebed that the motorcycles will come, pulverizing the cracked earth and raising a terrible dust. They will come in a roar of souped-up engines and a cloud like an approaching sandstorm. Until they thud to a halt in a tight half-circle and the whirlwind stills, you will not be able to see the riders clearly, and this is the way they want it. Until they lift the face plates you will not know who they are. Even then the riders' features will be obscured, frosted with desert sand, so that until their leader speaks you will not know her, and the lettering on the helmets? Not yet clear.

Bikes start: HUDN-HUDN. RMMM RMMM RMMMM. The leader raises a gauntleted hand: everybody here? Fifteen other bikers raise their hands for the count. *Ready*.

RMMM RMMMM RMMMMMMM. Watch out for them. The Little Sisters of the Apocalypse.

2

Although it's been five years the women of Schell Isle still think of themselves in relation to the men: —how they love him, how much they miss him. What his absence has done to them. Expecting the Return, they pine or grumble, and they could not tell you from one second to the next which they are doing now. They could not say whether they expect to rush out and welcome him—or arm the barricades. Without him cluttering up their minds—marked by the empty bed, the abandoned favorite chair—what triumphs and masterpieces would the women have room for? He built this place. His absence defines them.

Whereas the approaching cyclists care nothing for men because they are fixed on Christ, whom they hope to live and pray well enough and hard enough in this world to encounter in the next—a next world of which they are confident. If you asked why this heaven-bent sexual autonomy enrages some people and scares others, the sisters would tell you it's because they fulfill an eschatological function. The vestigial black habit, the shadow of the crucifix speak of last things. In chapel with their veils pulled over their faces at the Communion, the riders' predecessors looked to these women like walking tombstones, and not a woman among the bikers minded this. But they won't bother you with last things.

They don't preach. They ride.

Stand in the road at the end of the causeway and feel the road trembling with distant vibrations. It will be days before the riders come into sight, black forms suspended in heat mirages that make it hard to know at first sight what is real and what is only reflection.

They will appear first as flecks so indistinct that you can't be certain whether those are dead trees you see shimmering in the bright middle distance, or motorcyclists zooming in on you in their fearsome wedge formation: The Little Sisters of the Apocalypse.

Educated by nuns, K. grew up thinking she could be anything she wanted. Before feminism, nuns were the first feminists. Because they never knew marriage and family responsibilities, nothing stood between the sisters and their work. No consciousness raising needed here. Sisters taught K. she could do anything she wanted.

Waking abruptly, Chag calls. "Is that you?"

All over the island, women wake in empty beds and stretch, thinking sleepily: *What do I want to do today?*

For once they listen to their own marching orders. There's nobody else in the world they need to check with. It gives them a sense of luxury and tremendous leisure.

It won't last long. There is *this* in the air, some change that makes them sit up abruptly. They set their mouths in anticipation, although none knows what is coming.

27

The women move uneasily from room to room without knowing what they're looking for. They find it necessary to check the calendar. Uneasily, they look over their shoulders.

He said he'd be back.

He didn't say when.

Something big is coming.

The Return? Nobody knows.

Maybe it's only a seismic disturbance, or an atmospheric one. Tornado? No problem. Impending earthquake? Fine. They prefer a logical explanation, something they can pass off: oh, it's only...

Is the barometer dropping or is it something else that makes me feel the way I do, disrupted and unsettled?

Some women will feel their mouths dry out as warmth spreads in their soft places.

Listen, it could be him.

Are you out there?

Fear makes others of the women swallow hard and look out from behind their curtains. Others run to the end of their docks, straining to see beyond the lake and the barrier to the bleached horizon.

What if he doesn't make it?

They want him back; they don't want him back. They do not know. They want him to be all right but they want to keep things as they are. When something's working, you don't like changes.

What began as loneliness has turned into freedom. The women of Schell Isle expanded in his absence. Now they are used to it.

❖

Disenfranchised. K's mother dies by degrees in beautiful Florida.

White sands, blue water. Silver skies. Green trees in midwinter.
One of her first symptoms is a loss of affect.

❖

Understand the island was created at some cost, and if the women don't know exactly what these costs were it is because, like the progress of the remote war, the men chose to keep their actions a secret.

Men have a genius for expediency.

Land had to be cleared, and cleared along with it were the original landholders. Deeds got lost. The old buildings were leveled by the wrecking ball. Bulldozers rolled over the shacks and only the builders know whether the occupants were given enough warning. Take no prisoners, the men said, when what they meant was: leave no survivors, and if in an enclave not far from here the original property owners still live and simmer, this is not a problem for the men. Out of sight out of mind, they say. Hearing them explain the women wondered: *Does that apply to me too?*

❖

Growing up with a grieving mother, K. committed this scrap of Byron to memory: "Love is to men a thing apart. 'Tis woman's whole existence." Sexist? Maybe. It explained a lot of things.

❖

The men of Schell Isle are too long gone.

Locating their women here, they were already planning the Great Escape, writing farewell speeches as they sited

29

million-dollar houses along the waterfront. They ousted the Outlaw family to build this posh colony and set prices high enough to keep out the undesirable element—uncomely squatters like the Outlaws, the poor or the unworthy. They installed gun emplacements on the point and designed coded cards to open the toll gates on the mainland.

The ultimate refinement of the gated community.

People like us, the men told them. No undesirables.

But, the women say, endlessly running to the window, *What are we like? What are we like anyway?* There's not a one of them who does not wonder: *What would we be if we didn't have you to think about?*

Set like jewels in this desert oasis for the privileged, they protect and maintain the men's jewel box with its cluster of white houses in the middle of the artificial lake. Never mind that the lake is dry. Sunlight crashes off the pale tile roofs of glistening waterfront houses all the same. In the town center, people do business in handsome offices and seductive clusters of shops.

—Our women will be safe here, the men told each other as they vied for the grandest houses.

—Our women will be protected.

—The women will *shut up* here.

Songs they sang on the eve of their departure.

Who could be discontent in the cathedral living room with sliding doors to the swimming pool on the marble terrace; who'd notice if love or life turned out to be less than perfect? Who could complain? Surrounded by opulence, who would notice that she'd been left behind like so much surplus luggage?

Think about her in this nice place you've made for her and count her safe. Well taken care of. Free of the exigencies of life in the savage city. Locked away from the demon lover, the Other Man who doesn't love war as much as we do, and stays behind so he can creep in during the night and take her away from you. Count her safe in this expensive citadel.

The men reckoned without the bitterness of the neglected.

❖

He's coming. He's not coming. He may be coming. He may not come after all. How many times have we run down to the end of the dock like this, and how many times have we dragged ourselves back in the house because he wasn't out there and we've had no sign from him? What shall we feel about this, relieved or heartbroken?

❖

The women would tell you life without men has its good points.

With the men away at a war so remote that even television pictures look as though they've been strained through cheesecloth and poorly reassembled, society hums along peacefully. On Schell Isle there are few delays and hardly any mechanical breakdowns, no rapes and no robberies. When storms blow up from the desert, severing power lines and smashing windows, teams restore power almost immediately, and in the absence of lawmen there seems to be little need for them; without men, the major threat to physical safety has been eliminated.

Take back the night and use it any way you want to. Nobody's lurking in the parking lot or the laundry room, ready to pounce; there's nobody waiting in the elevator or hiding in the shadows of your living room, ready to spring out and force himself upon you. The women have settled in to a life without risk—or almost without risk. Taking off their shoes at night after a long day at business, walking barefooted in their thickly carpeted living rooms, they relax without straining to hear the unexpected footfall, the rattle of the marauder at the window.

The women are alone on Schell Isle except for Squiggy, the jack-of-all-trades who does their carpentry and tends bar at their parties, and Kitten Joe, the forbidding solitary with burned-out eyes who stalks the unpopulated part of the island, leaving a sinuous, glossy wake that hisses along in the sand behind him, stirring the dead grass as, mesmerized, dozens of cats of all shapes and sizes follow.

The women are alone on the island except for Squiggy, whom they use, and therefore despise, and Kitten Joe, who is a tightly locked secret.

They expand in the absence.

Yet in spite of this the slightest sound can make her wonder. Is he really gone? Is he gone for good this time?

Or is he only out at the corner convenience store, buying a pack of cigarettes?

Seeing somebody else?

Is he just about to come in and say, Salad and cake? Is that all we're having for dinner?

❖

K. spent one year in a girls' boarding school and four in a women's college.

32

❖

Is it OK to say life has been easier since the Departure?

It isn't the silence that pleases them, the women realize; it is rather the sense of *space*. Enough room in the bed. Enough room in the house. Enough room in their lives for once. They can go from back of the house to front unchallenged. Walk around in their pajamas if they feel like it. Neglect their hair. For the first time in their lives they don't have to please anybody. Things stay where they put them. The women are safe from domestic fights that flare up like flash fires, safe from nonspecific guilt and recriminations. Smeared jam and crumpled napkins. Crumbs on the kitchen table.

Leave the world to children and they will revert to savagery; they split into factions and create false gods. Leave the world to women and everything runs smoothly. Systems form and perfect themselves.

❖

Systems.

The flip side of every blessing is a curse. In the presence of the unbidden, inescapable ability to organize, women are, alas, masters of the location of small objects.

Such habits of mind are not easily broken.

Chag thinks, *We don't* want *to know these things*.

With one question, Toby can bring her down: "Honey, where's my other blue sock?" The hell of it was never his asking. It was that no matter how far her mind was roaming the minute before, how high she was vaulting, she always came back to give him the answer. She always knows and she hates it.

These are some of the things Chag knows without wanting to:

Where the bills are and what is owed on each.

Where the cufflink rolled after it bounced off the dresser.

Where the bodies are buried.

In ordinary times she knows exactly where on the kitchen shelf Toby will find the poppyseed, even as she knows that once he's done cooking, she'll have to clean up the kitchen.

Unwilling, Chag has this thrust upon her, the woman's genius, unless it is indeed a curse: the sure knowledge of the location of small objects. Every single one of them.

The fact that no matter what else she has in her mind, no matter what artistic problems trouble her, that she needs time and space to solve, Chag always knows what needs doing before she can get down to doing what she wants to do.

What could I not think if my mind wasn't filled up with all this useful junk? What could I not imagine?

Left to herself, Chag would be that poet, but shit, her mind is so cluttered that all that comes is doggerel. For a long time now she has projected a verse cycle, which she associates with the end of her responsibilities to the outside world. The minute Toby gets back she ditches this job and gets to it.

What stands between her and her unwritten work, she thinks, is this job as Acting Governor. She's so busy with systems, the duties of office and the need to organize her colleagues and complete the men's abandoned projects that she hasn't managed to write much. What Chag can't figure out is whether it's the details of the job that hold her back or the absence of Toby. She misses the presence, the simple fact of the extra bulk in the bed. The fact that when she speaks there's somebody else in the room to answer.

Look. She could always bag work and write, but she has commitments here.

Listen. There is this about the community of women. Rivals spring up like dragons' teeth. Let down for one minute and Courtney will come rushing in. Courtney, who goes to extremes.

Although she never asked for this, Chag will defend her position.

❖

See how Toby Hagen consolidated Chag's position. The car was waiting outside; his outlines blurred with departure. Leaving for war, he stopped long enough to take her face in his two hands. he said, "I'm going to win this for you."

"But I never asked you to fight it."

He silenced her with kisses, sugar-coating objections with the pervasive sweetness of last times, while just beneath the surface ran the savage current of superiority. "Hold the fort," he said.

Oh Toby. "Let me go with you."

"You know I can't." Toby, filled with importance. This is how he dismissed their life together. *Don't try to stop me. Do know you can't follow me. Never mind where I'm going, never mind how exotic it is or how dangerous, you can't come along and you can't even presume to know what I'm doing there, much less what it's like. I love you, but your place is here.*

Full of it: Man things. "You could get hurt." *You could be killed.* If he took me along, she thought, I could protect him.

Then she realized that wasn't it. No, that wasn't the whole it. *If he took me along at least I'd know what he was doing.*

Toby, who held her in place and said, "I'll be fine. I love

you, Chag. I can get through this as long as I know you're waiting."

"If you loved me you'd stay."

A horn hooted: the impatient driver. "I have to go now." This is how he dismissed her. "I'll be back," Toby said with that loving grin that levels Chag, quite simply flattens her. They all say that. The hell of it is, there's no way of knowing whether they believe it.

Although Chag hates Shakespeare, the words come up like flash cards: Is it in our men or is it something in ourselves that make us underlings? She is hung up on the paradox, the yang-yin relationship that refuses to explain itself. She wants to deal with this in her unwritten book of poems.

So far she has only the last line, which she keeps secret, and the title, which she claims here, for good and forever: ROAD KILLS.

❖

In the sharp shadow cut by the bright desert light on the sand below Chag's bedroom balcony, a dark figure lurks, hunched under the black slouch hat that hides everything—thought, yearning, expression. Without knowing what he's been waiting for, he has been waiting. Some inner mechanism clicks. A chunk of darkness, he separates himself from the larger shadow and, turning pale, blasted eyes toward the desert sun, slouches away unobserved. Smaller fragments of darkness slide into the white glare and follow. It is the reclusive Kitten Joe with his spume of cats streaming behind him, but Chag won't know this. If Chag knew he'd passed the better part of the day standing guard there it would unnerve her. But even if somebody told her about the silent vigil, she would not credit it.

None of the women knows what drives Kitten Joe any more than anyone knows what brought him here—a sense of mission? A command from a power they can't even guess at? Who can say? Whatever he's about, he's been here since the beginning, man-without-a-name who will not speak and turns away if he sees you coming. This is how they assess him: Solitary. Ruined. Harmless. Those who have come close enough to see under the hat brim say he looks destroyed, like a burned-out house or a flier who's come too close to the sun, Kitten Joe, who in ordinary circumstances keeps to the overgrown, secret part of the island.

His presence here is an anomaly.

The living shadow moves away followed by its train of silent, sinuous little shadows, and if Chag does not see that Kitten Joe's been here underneath her balcony, it's just as well.

Even if she did look out; even if she saw, her orderly mind would discount it, reorganizing the information: *Oh, it's only Squiggy.*

❖

Preening in her bedroom in the next house, Courtney Ravenal hears a stir as the last cat rounds the corner. She springs to the window, but too late to see anything but the flick of a shadow. It's gone so fast that she can't even be sure it's there. Something, she thinks and then—wishful thinking?—with an excited shiver she thinks: Something bad is coming down.

Although she's supposed to be Chag's trusted lieutenant and her acting chief of police, a secret, ugly part of Courtney is dancing with excitement. What if there really is something malign out there, that will eliminate Chag for her?

Like the Wicked Witch Courtney thinks, *Then I will be the fairest in the land*. Or does she mean: *the strongest*.

❖

Are you just going to let them take it away from you?

❖

In a barrio in a burned-out city too close to Schell Isle to be completely safe for the women's colony but too far away for them to be aware of it, the Outlaw family stirs in a tangle of bodies. One by one they begin to wake.

Huge, hairy and malodorous, Queenie sprawls at the center.

The loft where the Outlaws moil in their blankets is rank and dismal, littered with broken glass and abandoned possessions left behind by the fleeing occupants—TVs with the tubes blown out, three-legged chairs and shattered china. The walls of the abandoned loft are crosshatched with graffiti and blackened by smoke from the Outlaws' cooking fires, but lined as it is with lush carpets smeared with grease and strewn with pillows redolent of their bodies it is luxuriously comfortable, more. It is theirs, and theirs entirely.

Confronted by the disorder, the women of Schell Isle would tsk-tsk and start shoveling out the rubble and replastering and painting, determined to make the nest over in their image, but the Outlaws could care less that to an outsider's eyes the place is disgusting. This is how they like it. It says something about the way they feel right now. If the

38

Outlaws are living here and not in the relocation communities the men designed to bribe them away from Schell Isle, it is for a reason.

Right before they killed him King Outlaw rose until he seemed bigger than he was, glaring and growling like a grizzly, "You can hurt us but you can't destroy us."

The leader of the advance detail said, "We're not trying to destroy you, we're trying to relocate you. Look at this splendid project we've built for you." He unfolded a map of an apartment block: living room, two bedrooms, uniform as white toast, everything homogenized.

Father of them all, King snarled, "Stash us in boxes."

"Man, look at the way you're living!" With a sweep of his hand the leader took in the shacks and rusted-out car bodies that made the Outlaw community.

"This is the way we live," King said, and he was proud of it.

The leader's face registered disgust and he let it show. This was his mistake. When he said, "You'll do better in the projects," the tone was all: There-There. Condescending. He did not add that it was Queenie and her daughters who would be stowed in apartment boxes; the Outlaw men would be chewed up in the maw of progress and spat out as soldiers.

King never gave them a chance. Rising up like Godzilla, ready to knock them flat with his scaly tail, Queen Outlaw's man, lover and light of her life, champion forager and the father of her family raised his assault weapon and charged the interlopers, roaring: "Fuck the project."

So they had to blow him away.

"Fuck no you won't move us," King cried as the first bullets tore into him. "No way." Howling, King rushed into the spray of fire until they finally cut him in two and even after that he was still screaming, "Nobody destroys us."

What he meant was: You're trying to change us. The Outlaws don't want to be changed. They are militantly what they are and proud of it: reckless and scuzzy, foul and free.

Change us and you destroy us.

Queenie saw it all and swore vengeance.

Mother of them all, Queenie Outlaw spreads at the center of the family constellation. See them sleeping: grown children, their mates and lovers and babies, an engine of sprawling flesh fueled by hatred. For the first time since King died, his widow wakes up smiling. Here in the tangle of soiled pillows and rich Oriental carpets, Queenie is flanked or supported by her favorites, her boys Lord and Earl and Prince, who's been the light of her life ever since her King died at the hands of the liars who evicted them.

Among men she has made, Queenie can be herself. Waking up among her sons and grandchildren, surrounded and reinforced by her own flesh, she is as close as it comes to happy.

But forever diminished because King is dead. Killed in the first engagement in the battle for Schell Isle. Fucking white-collar bastards with their fucking candyfaced bitches.

King Junior died in the skirmish too, leveling his assault weapon at all comers even as his father reeled backward with his gun still vomiting bullets. Within days Queenie's sweet-eyed, unsuspecting baby Duke was snagged off by Army recruiters and shipped to the front and killed in the war before Queenie even realized they had him. The telegram said Duke was dead, but you couldn't trust the Army.

How has Queenie hidden her other sons from recruiters? In fact, she didn't have to. Her older sons are so big, so mean and so ugly that nobody would dare come near them.

Nobody. The Outlaw boys are like their fathers, stout as grizzlies, tall, hairy and powerful. You think they're dangerous on their own? It's like toying with tiger cubs. Touch them and you bring down the mother.

Earl is too big and strong to argue with and Lord sleeps with a knife between his teeth. Count flies into dangerous rages. Cross him and you do not walk away, any more than you walk away from Baron. Unlike the others, Queenie's favorite is graceful and light-boned, tawny and fair as a lion cub: Prince, who hears things ordinary people don't hear and sees things they can't even guess at.

Prince, who is touched by a power Queenie senses but can't name. *Oh please*, she says, to what occult agency she doesn't know. *Please don't take my baby*, Queenie says because even though Prince is hurled through life by something beyond her comprehension, she can feel the presence of whatever drives him. *Something outside us*.

And when it seizes him, she backs off until it is over.

Slighter than his brothers, Prince is formidable. He can without warning electrify enemies by pitching a fit. His eyes roll; his arms fly and he charges anybody who crosses him with the strength of the unspeakable. Shout his name and he won't hear you. Tranquilizer darts don't slow him and even bullets won't stop him: some wild Yogic concentration protects him; in a gentler civilization Prince would walk on fire, but the times are not gentle.

No wonder everybody is afraid of the Outlaws. Even the tough, stringy boys who married Queenie's daughters are wary. Nobody messes with the Outlaws because the wild red light flickering behind the eyes makes it clear: they don't care. Do not give a fuck. These people will do anything.

Together in the loft, Queenie's daughters Duchess, Princess and Lady lie close to the center with their own mates, rejected by society but cherished here in the fortress of family. The Outlaw women are drawn to tightly muscled, murderous punks with hair-trigger tempers.

This is the family developers were foolish enough to drive away from the land they consider their birthright.

Men, Queenie thinks. Always men. In the kingdom of the blind, Queenie would be as cute as anyone. She saw the looks on the faces of the men who evicted her. The insult was not being hunted down and routed like snakes and it wasn't in being lied to. It was the contempt with which the men of Schell Isle leveled the shanties. In spite of King's antitank guns and the BARs, the advance detail moved in with bulldozers, tipping shacks, ready to smash anything that ran out from underneath. To them it was like flushing roaches.

And when she came out with her hands up... Queenie will never forgive the looks on their faces: *ugly. Man, this woman is ug-lee.*

Well damn you all to hell and back, she thinks.

Queenie has lived with this insult for nearly six years and with the other, deeper insult for a lifetime. Seeking justice in the matter of the one, she will wreak vengeance for the other.

Ask Queenie what she's doing and she will tell you about the projected raid on Schell Isle. "Taking back what's ours," she says.

But there is more to it.

Over the years Queenie has husbanded her strength and gathered her forces. She's stolen trucks and stockpiled weapons. The Indians got their land back in good time and now people call them Native Americans. So will the Outlaws. And what will people call them? Like the Apache gods, Queenie is vengeful and powerful, and like them, she is tireless.

42

Ask her to give you her real reason for the raid and she will take your arm off at the elbow.

"Up," she says. "This is it." When people stir and grumble but don't wake Queenie takes a bullhorn off the wall and says: "Today's the day."

Queenie galvanizes her family, speaking in the steely voice of the disenfranchised and displaced everywhere. "Time to move!"

Then something unsettling happens. If the Outlaws lived in a movie it would be the camera tilting so that people, setting, life itself goes out of kilter. Queenie is aware of a momentary shift or disruption in the atmosphere.

She lifts her head and falls silent, breathing hard.

She isn't sure, but she thinks she hears it: RMMM RMMM RMMMMMM. The vibration of many motors.

She whirls. "What the fuck is that!"

And one by one her Baron and Princess, Count and Lady, Duchess—everybody but Prince says, "I don't hear anything."

Outraged, she lashes out, hitting three of her children in one sweep. "What the fuck do you mean, you don't hear it?"

There is a silence. Then she looks at Prince. Looking through or beyond her he speaks to someone or something else: "You called?" His voice is strange, remote, hollow.

She shouts. "What? What is it?"

With his pale green irises spinning Prince stands, rising like a pale flame out of the center of the mass of bodies. He hangs in place with his arms spread and his mouth wide, as if waking from a profound dream. The afterimage rivets him. Something hangs in the air between him and his mother. What? He is fixed on it.

Too much time goes by before Prince shakes himself and

43

the part of him that has gone out returns to them.

"I don't know."

Arrested by the presence of something he acknowledges but does not yet recognize, Queenie Outlaw's dearest son the visionary, Prince, who has always been strange, says in hushed tones, "I don't know yet."

❖

Loss of affect precedes the death of K.'s mother by some years, in an inexorable advance that destroys personhood. In narrative, in life? K. builds strong women.

❖

RMMM, RMMM. On one of the highways of life, the mystery cyclists hit top speed. Wind sneaks into their black jackets and makes them billow. Like the writing on the wall, the silver crosses glint on their black helmets. The others may not yet have their orders but the leader knows where they are going; they are heading west toward the desert and Schell Isle, in a state so far away that it will take them days to get there.

Trini rides point. Sister Trinitas, who has been called to lead the group on this mission. Next come Agatha and Perpetua, followed by Celeste Marie, Virtua and Lucy. Fanning out behind them are the others, hard-riding women hell-bent on God, whom they pursue as if they expect to find Him somewhere on the hard road ahead of them. They are sixteen in all, an order of religious who wear motorcycle jackets over the vestigial habits—black jeans, white blouses, black scarves that conceal and signify the neck chain and swinging crucifix: the Little Sisters of the Apocalypse.

Sister Trinitas rides her rebuilt Harley '74 with the chrome wheels and the raccoon tails streaming; she took it in the Melee of '00, from a dying biker. Dipping her hand into a puddle, she gave him conditional baptism and stayed long enough to close his eyes and say a final prayer over him.

Next to God, Trini loves her bike. Although she would not confess it to the others because she knows it is irrational, she rides along with her heart thudding and her mouth cracked in a vaulting, unquenchable hope. Never mind the computers with their speed and their slippery certainty. Never mind the hours she steals from sleep so she can meditate. When she is roaring along like this, swift and free and filled with aspiration, Trini cannot suppress the idea that if she can just get going fast enough, or in a true enough line or in the right spirit; if she can only ride a pure line on the highway of life she may hit Mach 4 and leap the requisite number of cars or span the appropriate gulf like a god struck Evel Knievel and at lightspeed encounter the eternal.

Sister Agatha's voice comes into her headphones, pulling her back to the physical present. "You know where we're going?"

The answer rocks Trini but she keeps her voice cool. "Yes. I do," she says. "Orders."

"From where?" Ag is as impatient as she is pragmatic.

"I can't say yet."

How is Trini going to tell Ag that all this—their mission—came to her in the night, with the clarity of a vision?

Ag's voice buzzes in Trini's helmet. "The least you can do is tell us why."

"I can't." The mystery fills her up. She says, "Bear with me?"

"Don't I always?" Ag's voice crackles. "You're sure this is important."

Trini says, "It had better be."

"What do you want me to tell the others?"

Trini does not answer. *Mach 4*, she thinks. *Sweet Holy Spirit.* She is intent on the outside possibility.

Ag's voice is stern. "Sister?"

"In a minute, Ag." Earthbound, Trini is put in her place by duty. She would like nothing better than to be a spark flying up, but in this community she is the Superior. She has her responsibilities. Struck by a bolt in the night, she came back to herself with the idea that this particular mission is something the sisters must undertake for its own sake. The true purpose will come clear in time, but Trini does not yet know it. She does not know how to put this. Then she does. "Tell them it's an exercise."

Ag's voice crackles in the phones. "A pilgrimage?"

She thinks: *spiritual exercise.* How to explain? She says, "More like maneuvers."

Literal-minded Ag won't let enough be enough. "Like the army?"

"Something we have to do," Trini says impatiently and shuts off her helmet radio.

In fact, they are riding to effect a rescue. Of whom? Trini is not sure. From what? That has not been revealed to her. She knows only that she has been given a sacred charge and she has no choice but to proceed, and without question.

3

Put yourself on Schell Isle now, where nothing is wrong, exactly, but where the air is unaccountably thin and empty. It is as if the island sits in a vacuum—the air hushed in anticipation of whatever force is rushing in to fill it. Although the riders are a thousand miles away and on Schell Isle nothing is really different, the texture of the island flexes and changes slightly to admit the possibility.

The earth vibrates.

• In her handsome house, Chag whips her head around: *You called?* There is no answer.

• Shut into his shack, a brilliant mind locked into this huge, crudely drawn body like diamonds in a safe without a combination, Kitten Joe squints into the middle distance. *What?* Twisting, the recluse starts to his feet in a joyful agony: *What, oh what!* He does not know what, only that something inside him has been touched and set twanging.

He paces with his mouth wide. *Please, what!* There is no answer; there's nobody there *to* answer. What is the stranger the women call Kitten Joe listening for, and what is he awaiting? The devil? The deity? Where was he before he landed on this island? If only he could remember!

Confusion makes his soul shudder. "Not worthy," Kitten

Joe says aloud, waiting for a door to close.

But the excitement will not leave him. He winces in pain as the mind he's shut away for so long stirs and quickens. Alone in a tremendous silence he shouts, "What do you want me to do?"

• Courtney Ravenal wakes, threatened by the vision of the man who left her behind here. Light of her life, betrayer, bastard. Robert. Everything in Courtney's body reaches out to him but in her mind and with all her will she pushes him away. "Think you can walk out and then walk right back in like you never left, do you?" She bares perfect teeth in a snarl. "Well I'll show you."

• Orphaned as a child in some other war, Verena puts down her father's photograph—God, he looks splendid in the uniform. She puts it down and in spite of the fact that Daddy has been missing for so long the Army's declared him officially dead, fresh expectations surprise her. It's not her husband's name Verena calls as the air quickens. The absent Matt never enters her mind as she rushes to the window.

When her voice rises, sweet and tremulous, it is to name the one who has been gone the longest. Verena, in hopes. "Daddy?"

❖

A. Alvarez writes: "The missing parent like an open wound." K. finds the durability of grief astounding.

❖

• From their beds in sickrooms located on opposite sides of the island, Stephanie, who may be dying of cancer, and Nella, who should be getting well after an overdose of sleeping pills, rise on their elbows.

Stephanie sighs. "Oh, Larry."

And Nella, who knows better, sits up with her teeth bared and her heart pounding in hope. "David?

The women are linked by their age and their state in life and proximate and remote causes of misery.

One woman is being pulled into death against her will and the other is reluctantly drifting away from it.

Nella tried to kill herself because her ex-husband David stopped loving her. The only scenario she can see is one in which she gets him back. Married for life and he loved somebody else, well she showed him, or she almost did. Vomiting up the pills, she woke from her long dream of death to find herself in a hospital room with Stephanie.

Steph shook her head in incomprehension. "Why would anybody die on purpose?"

"My pride," Nella explained. It is so obvious!

"My breasts," Stephanie said. "Just so I can stay alive!" The surgery was complete and completely disfiguring.

Both women said in the same voice, "Think what a thing like this can do to your pride."

Nella said, "I didn't take enough."

At the same time Steph groaned, "They didn't get it all."

Now they are home from the hospital. Nella wants to get it over with. All Stephanie wants is to live to see Larry. In a more lenient order of things, the women might be able to change places.

Aware of the difference in the air, Stephanie mistakes it for approaching death, crying, "Not yet! I have things to do!"

Death. Surprised and relieved, Nella holds out her arms to the intruder she is certain must be death, saying thickly as if to a long-awaited lover, "You came after all."

49

Nurses pop into the doorways of both women's bedrooms: hospice nurse in the one case, assigned to help
Stephanie die, suicide watch instructed to drag her patient
back to life in Nella's. Both nurses say, "You want something?"

For her own reasons, each woman lies. Stephanie touches
the sore spot and says, "It's nothing."

Smiling brightly, Nella deceives her guard. "It's nothing."

• And in his trailer down by the dump, restless, loathesome
Squiggy awakes to guilty joy. The weapon in the closet. The
body in the ditch. The satisfaction. Alone among the women
and damn them all, nobody wants him; lust tortures him.
Have I already done it, or did I only dream it? But except for the
disturbance in the air everything is the same here.

Uneasy, he calls out. "All right, for God's sake. Who's out
there?"

Sheee-sh! No answer.

❖

*In an unexpected race with K.'s mother, two of K.'s close friends
are also dying: A., who does not want to leave her life, and M., who
was brought back from death once by heroic measures and is not
happy about it. She's weighing her options. "Stick around," K.
says. "I don't know," M. says, although she's already decided.
"I'm thinking about it."*

❖

Aware, feeling guilty over her own obscene good health in
the face of Steph's illness and Nella's misery, Chag is dogged
by another piece of doggerel:

In the room the women come and go
Talking of ways to die, you know?

❖

Large shapes chase each other across the skies above Schell Isle; nothing you can see, exactly. Not clouds, not planes or even vapor trails. Instead the silvery skies are filled with afterimages, as if something big has passed through unseen.
Signs?
Wonders?
It's too early to tell.
The air quickens with possibilities.

❖

Nobody knows it is the cyclists coming.
Chag imagines the disturbance has something to do with the men returning: *Toby!* Never mind that things run smoother without him; she misses him in her heart and soul and body. *Who? Who is it?* But when she goes to her post on the balcony she sees nothing out there and nothing coming.
Although Chag is wired into police computers on the island, although she has just received a garbled radio transmission—a threat from the Outlaw family? Something better? Worse?—she has nothing concrete to go on.
She'd like to call someone, talk to somebody she trusts— *Do you hear it too?* and have that person say, There There, but the exclusivity of her close marriage has beggared her.
You have little need for other people when your best friend is the man you're sleeping with.
Toby didn't leave much room in her life for friends. When

51

he left, the job rushed in to fill her thoughts and take her best energies. There's nobody Chag can go to right now. She sometimes feels like the only person left alive on this island in the desert. This desert island.

Friends, she thinks. I need friends. And faces this fact: her only true friend in the world is Toby. *Oh God*, she thinks. *Don't let anything happen to Toby*.

She understands at the same time that it's possible that it's not the soldiers, it's the women who are in danger. A potential attack? From within, or without? She does not know.

Protected as they are by the sealed houses, by the toll gates and the electronic barrier, Chag wants to think that they on the island are proof against whatever's out there.

❖

They've all forgotten about Squiggy.

❖

It's not seeing that these women have all the power that makes his life so miserable, Squiggy thinks: it's that powerful women are the majority. Who wouldn't hate them? Give or take a couple of ancient gentlemen in the island's one rest home, forgotten patriarchs—and always excepting Kitten Joe—Squiggy is the only man still living on Schell Isle—at least the only man who still has to work for a living.

Not much of a man, it would appear, Squiggy with his ferret's slouch and his scarred face veiled by what he imagines is a glamorous stubble. What the women don't reckon with is the strength in those stringy arms, the amazing chest muscles because Squiggy secretly works out when he isn't doing their bidding. Equipment bought from a defunct shopping channel litters the bedroom of the ugly little trailer. One day soon when he's strong enough, he's going to swoop down and surprise them.

Sitting in his trailer by the dump, Squiggy counts his money and reflects on the injustice. The trailer is neatly kept in spite of the absence of subservient babes to scrub his counters and put fresh toilet paper in his bathroom. Squiggy makes up for this lack by surrounding himself with women's pictures. His walls are plastered with them: old centerfolds and high school graduation photographs and wedding pictures filched from the houses where he's worked along with Polaroids he has taken at night, pictures of careless women undressing by open windows.

When he isn't at work Squiggy maintains constant phone contact with potential employers, honeying up to the women in the one circumstance in which they just may forget what he looks like and talk that nice, slick talk to him. Anything to get him to work for them. Some of those bitches get so excited talking to a man that they forget who he is and treat him like a handsome, or is it inoffensive-looking guy instead of just Squiggy, that came out from under some rock somewhere that they keep around because they need him.

And then they look: *Oh, it's only. Ugh! Squiggy.*

Squiggy both loves and hates the women. He hates them because he is Squiggy and they are the masters.

He loves them because in these times, in their circumstances, he is the best they can get. Women need Squiggy and he needs them, and when this thing is over he'll be rich enough to buy one of the best houses. He gets paid for odd jobs the men might have done if they'd stayed around long

53

enough. The women need him to polish brass and silver in their expensive houses while they put on three-piece suits and go off to business; they need him to set up for their parties and put on his white coat and make drinks and pass hors d'oeuvres to important clients who blow into town on business, and to trap desert rats for them because women may be powerful, but in the presence of anything that scuttles, they are only women. They need Squiggy to do things too disgusting or dull for them to bother with, dispose of vermin, clean up sewage overflows and toxic spills and drag away palm branches after every desert storm.

It's ugly work, some of it. Squiggy needs the money. He also needs the women to sleep with him. Not many will but just occasionally somebody does, some tired hostess who's drunk a little too much may turn to him over the ranks of dirty glasses on the drinks table, and try to forget what he looks like. She may close her eyes or open her dress in a weary show of inevitability, for which he despises her. Once, OK? It's only happened once, but never mind.

You can travel a long way on possibilities.

The possibility alone is enough to make life feasible for Squiggy, who has never been able to get work in the real world be cause of the way he looks and the way he *is*: avid, greasy, feral. So in this closed community he does the women's dirty work and shows his pointed teeth in a servile smile and occasionally relieves himself in a lady's underwear drawer or spirits away certain ancestral silver when he thinks she isn't looking.

"He's marvelous," the women say when he has lofted trays of *hors d'oeuvres* at a particularly elegant party or stood behind the hostess's chair at a smoothly-managed dinner. The hostess will praise Squiggy and overpay him and pass him on to the next hostess. Because she cannot afford to brook or admit mistakes of any kind she will forget or ignore that funny smell in her dresser or the creepy feeling that some of her silver is missing and she'll pass him on to the next hostess: "He's absolutely wonderful," she'll say, in the conviction that this is absolutely true. Women speak so highly of him that each woman knows if there's something at all wrong in her relationship with this employee the fault must be with herself, not Squiggy, "Absolutely. You'll love Squiggy."

❖

The shack on the point seethes with life. It is as if the palmettos and scrub pines have taken on legs and tails and begun moving. If you look closely at the vegetation you will see that it's not the trees that are moving; it's the hundreds of creatures clinging to them. Cats stir in the branches and spring upon small creatures fleeing through the long grasses. Cats twine around Kitten Joe, licking the caked areas where the soles of his shoes meet the cracked leather uppers and knotting their bodies in sinuous ropes that rise about his legs in garlands from the ankles; cats perch on every beam and shelf of his hut and hang from every supporting member. He has only to speak to stir a panic in the mass of furry bodies; he has only to open the door and walk out to start a tidal wave as they surge out to follow him.

If his sad face is puzzled, bemused, only the cats see. Only the cats see that he is destroyed from within, as if scarred by some terrible psychic accident.

Only the cats know the recluse does not know who he used to be or why he has been put here.

55

The sinister slouch and the knifeblade profile keep the women at a distance; nobody wants to come near enough to see the true color of the hooded eyes beneath the crumpled hat brim or to see his face naked and read the expression.

Nobody knows where Kitten Joe came from or who he is or what he hopes for in the ultimate scheme of things and because they don't understand, they're afraid of him, when in fact it is Squiggy they should be afraid of. And Kitten Joe? What is he afraid of?

Not knowing what's needed when it's finally needed.

❖

Looking at a snapshot of her estranged husband Matt, Verena knows it's time to forget him. Not his fault that he told her it was goodbye for good right before he marched away from her. "I'm sick of competing with your father."

When I was five, she thinks, Daddy gave me a new pencil with the silhouette of his destroyer on it in silver. Then he put his cap on my curls and told me to wait and I didn't know why Mother was crying.

Yes I waited.

Once an orphan, always an orphan, Verena thinks and can not tell you why it's still so painful.

Sometimes when she and Matt made love she could hear her own voice calling, "Daddy!" When I was five she thinks and then cries out and doubles over because even now, a lifetime later, loss twists in her like the right key in a rusty lock, tearing at her belly: *Oh! That poor little girl!*

She begged Matt not to go. "Not again," she said, "I can't go through this again," and couldn't admit to herself why she never let herself get too attached to him.

56

And going to this new war Verena's husband Matt said bitterly, "If you want to know the truth, I can't wait to get out of here." This then, is how he reproached her. "I'm sick of having your father in bed with us!"

✤

It's not men, I hate, Courtney Ravenal thinks bitterly. It's what they make of me.

Her situation is both the same and dead opposite to Queenie's. Furious as she is, exiled and resentful, Queenie is in her own way defined by the men who did this. Not so much because they killed her husband King and wrecked her nest as because she saw revulsion in their faces when they looked at her.

Unlike Queenie, who is what she is, Courtney is too beautiful.

Courtney's curse, if it is a curse, is that she looks like society's idea of perfection. It's a fulltime job in itself.

In other circumstances they might be allies.

In her own way, beautiful Courtney is just as bitter. She'd like to be able to let her hair go to seed and wear the same clothes for days on end; she'd like to wear bed socks to work and—OK, gain eight thousand pounds, but she worked too hard bringing her self to this perfect state: near-starvation, exercise beyond the point of exhaustion. The plastic surgeon yanked out two ribs and fixed the line of her jaw and as she lay there writhing said, *a simple little procedure.* She'd like to let it all go but she doesn't know how. She's forgotten what living with a full ribcage is like and she's forgotten her real nose and the original line of her jaw. Get somebody who's willing to put her face back the way it was and she won't be

57

able to remember it. She can't go a day without working out and all these years later she still can't look at chocolates without vomiting.

She'd like to let herself go but she can't. The inner discipline is too strongly entrenched.

Like it or not, Courtney hears her mother. *Darling, your hair! What if he saw you like this?*

Even without the men here to see and judge, Courtney is superbly turned out. Her hair is perfect. She tells herself that looking good is good for business, but in her heart she knows that she dresses to kill because she hates what she needs. A part of her is always looking ahead to the next man and a part is always looking over her shoulder to see what the last one thought of her.

In spite of her strength and emotional toughness, in spite of her marksmanship and her skill at management, she still depends on men even as she hates them. In the absence of her mother the perfectionist, they are her mirrors. She does not exist without their approval. She hasn't seen herself reflected in the eyes of any man—not since the Departure.

She will arm-wrestle rivals to death and throw acid in Chag's face if she has to, anything to win because Courtney is hungry, driven, flawed. She hates the men but she needs it. She needs to see herself mirrored in their eyes.

And she needs to win. It makes no sense. It's all she cares about. Without Robert here to bear witness Courtney is like an actor immobilized by the lack of audience or the tree in the quad, failing to fall because there are no onlookers.

Fuck, dammit, dammit, fuck! Who needs this?

Courtney knows she drove Robert away with her lust for admiration, her need to be best at everything. She scared him to death! Leaving for the war, her lover looked back at her

58

and waved goodbye with such a grin of relief that Courtney will never forgive him. He was ready to get killed. Death was no problem. Robert would do anything to free himself from the pressure of her expectations.

No wonder she wants to kill them all.

Then she can get on with the business at hand: ousting Chag—*now I will be the fairest in the land*. Or does she mean, *the strongest.*

When she's dressed and made herself up to glossy perfection, Courtney goes to the indoor rifle range and fires round after round. Filled to exploding with rage, she bubbles with it. *Take that, Robert. For being afraid of me.* WHAM.

She doesn't want to be this way, she thinks: WHAM.

Hates feeling this way: POW.

Has to end it: SPLAT.

Has to get her rocks off: WHAM. Release the rage: POW. SPLAT: Do violence. CRASH: kill them all.

It's the only way, she thinks. No. She knows. *Get rid of them.*

Courtney would be the first to tell you men have made her what she is. Perfected, she's the beautifully tooled monster, smooth and gorgeous. Waiting to go haywire.

Some of K.'s friends go to The Hall of New Faces. The results do not make her envious but she thinks, Hey wait. Would I? Knows she won't. Then why can't she stop thinking about it?

Riding along at the head of the pack, letting her bike howl as she splits the wind, Trini could have told poor orphaned

Verena it was not Daddy she missed, OK? She could have told Courtney it was not the approval of the men that she hated, no, loved, no, needed. That all her needs stand for something bigger, wider, wilder.

Trini would have identified it as the pressure of the eternal.

The hunger in all of us.

It is this hunger that she devotes her life to assuaging, Trini, who comprehends the thunderous absence. She welcomes it. Painful as it is, she sometimes thinks that it's the only proof she has that there is something out there.

Understand what it's like to send your mind out, to strip it of vanity and will and give up everything you have in an attempt to empty it and then speed forth without knowing what you will encounter—

No.

Without knowing whether you will encounter it.

Get comfortable on your knees, not so comfortable that you fall asleep or daydream; get uncomfortable and try to empty yourself in hopes that you can create the deep stillness in which you may see or hear or sense the eternal.

The profound hush into which it can fall, but only when you have emptied yourself of any hope of it.

This is the true business of the Little Sisters of the Apocalypse. Community of sisters, contemplatives, bikers all, they speed on together, hurtling into eternity.

In a conversation about something else K.'s friend, who is a religious, accidentally touches on meditation. She says in her off-hand way: "After four or five hours you get kind of tired."

❖

Agatha is sprinting now; she's come abreast of Trini and is tapping her helmet and shouting. Trini can see her friend's agitated face through the plexi faceplate and reluctantly flicks the switch so she can hear what Ag is saying into her radio: "Food," Ag says. "Rest."

Instead of speaking Trini responds with a sweeping wave that sends them forward, marking the way with her gloved index finger. Keep going! Keep going west!

"Why?"

Because I have to.

"Tired," Ag shouts. "Angry," she says.

Trini switches on her mike. "Love!"

"Getting pissed."

Trini says, "The discipline."

"Enough's enough," Ag says and then lowers her voice as if that will somehow keep the others from knowing what she is saying.

The word rushes into Trini's helmet: mutiny.

Trini is used to making command decisions. "The next town," she says. "There's a priory."

"Not a minute too soon," says Ag.

"But I don't think we should stay long. I don't know what this is," Trini confesses to the old friend who joined the convent in the same year she did. Good old Ag, who would follow her anywhere. "I don't know what we have to do when we get there and I don't know why," she says to her second in command. "But I know our mission is urgent."

❖

While in a remote part of the island Squiggy completes certain dirty business.

4

It may be...

Surrounded by the women of her community, Trini considers. God, I have to do this. God help me get it right. She has just come from an interview with the abbot.

With their helmets off and their scarves loosened, the Little Sisters of the Apocalypse sit on the flagstones with their arms resting on their knees and their sweet, grave faces pinkened by the heat from the fire. They are relaxed, expectant. There's so much she needs to tell them!

The time has come for an explanation. She frames the sentence with great care.

It may be that we are riding in for the convergence that comes at the end of the world.

Trini is not trying to buck up her colleagues, exactly; she is trying to make sense of it. She and the others have raced through clouds of boiling yellow smoke from the remote front where the army goes about its grim business. They've covered hundreds of miles of blasted countryside on their way to the impending rendezvous; they have rolled through the main streets of deserted burned-out cities with streets lined by the empty shells of destroyed lives. They've fared forward through sleet and weathered a hail of cinders followed by an ugly green rain. Riding west, they have passed bleached upturned ribcages rocking in the sand and animals with scorched fur skulking across the ruined landscape.

Signs and wonders? They've seen plenty. Yet Trini can't find the words for what may be coming. She can only address what they may be expected to do.

"It may be," Trini begins, but finds she's still not ready to launch this.

The sisters are sitting around their fire in the crumbling cloister of a nearly deserted priory, eating a dinner made from their own provisions and fresh fruit and vegetables the abbot gave them after he had shown Trini the computer lab.

At the end of their interview she'd said to the abbot, "We're alike, aren't we?"

At eighty, the old monk was at home with this. "In the eyes of God we are all alike," he said.

Like the Little Sisters of the Apocalypse, the monks run programs on their computers in an incessant search for a route into the mystery. Probabilities unfold and duplicate; the models they devise spin out millions of options and the options mutate and repeat in a dozen different computer languages. By ringing changes on the several million possible for names for God, the monks hope to arrive at the right one.

❖

This may even be possible. We take on the speed of the analog mind. With the computer we can move faster than light, faster than thought; sophisticated programs leapfrog the first stages of almost every thought process, hurtling us along. Note the mobility. Note the multiplicity of options.

Think about the purity of concentration. Sit down to work on something you really care about: the problem you need to solve or the world you are creating. Devised to serve you, your computer pulls you into your work. You miss appointments. You forget lunch. You burn dinner. Walk into what you are doing and when you come out—the phone rings; someone touches your shoulder—you will be astounded by how much time has escaped you. *How did it get so late so fast?*

Where did the time go while you were thus engaged? Did it go somewhere else?

Or did you?

It is this possibility that the monks and the Little Sisters of the Apocalypse are pursuing—the perfection of abstraction.

❖

If her mother's illness began with loss of affect, that was not nearly so terrifying to K. as phase two, the loss of reason. Powerless before the relentless, apparently random brutality, K. finds it necessary to impose order.

❖

The abbot grieves because the few monks remaining at the priory are old. He tells Trini there are no novices. With the war and the dearth of new candidates there are only a dedicated handful of old men left here. When this last generation dies the computers will run on and on with no new monks to attend them—or to note when God enters the solution. The few survivors man the terminals and pray in sequence in the ruined chapel so that at no time will their business go unattended: their lovingly minute exploration of relationship of the people of God and their creator.

"In times like these," the abbot explained ruefully as he and Trini backed out of the computer lab, "it's hard for the young to see the beauty of the discipline. We've lost quite a few, some to secular life and some some to the war."

"The war." Trini shakes her head. "Willful destruction. It doesn't make sense."

"Belfast. Beirut. Bosnia. Boston. The noise in their heads gets so loud it drowns out everything else," the abbot said. "But the monks who left so they could go to war are not our gravest loss. One of our best and—is it all right to say holiest? One of our best men..." His pale eyes clouded with regret.

Without knowing where the name came from Trini said, "Jerome?"

The abbott turned quickly but did not ask how she knew. "Yes. Jerome. So bright, so close to breaking through." The abbot held his torch to the wall of the gallery outside the chapel. Commanding, mysterious, the lost monk's likeness was chalked there on the stone. So strange! It was like looking into the face of a long-lost twin brother. "Tragic."

"I know it was."

"He got too close!" The abbot sighed. "He burned too bright, and then..."

Moved and unaccountably shy, Trini knew what he meant and would not name it: the fire that touches her and sends her yearning into the unknown. *Mach 4*. It seemed too private to talk about. Instead she said, "What happened?"

"We don't know. He got too close to something and it combusted. Consumed him from the inside out."

Not lukewarm, Trini thought, but she said, "I'm sorry."

"I know you are. Then he disappeared." The abbot sighed. "Just wandered out into the wasteland."

"There will be others," Trini said without conviction. There are no young men left in this place.

"Who can we find to replace him? The young don't want this. They're full of lust and fire. These days it's hard to attract the new generation. For even the holiest," he said sadly, "sex seems to be a problem."

(Trini was more amused than surprised: and they say *women* are too physical—not worthy to offer the Mass, to baptize and forgive, when what they mean is: all that blood, you are too dirty. Right.) "Oh, really?"

He caught her look and cleared his throat. "Well. If you'll excuse me, Sister."

❖

"The next time somebody tries to kill the pope," one of K.'s nun friends said, and she was not altogether joking, "It's going to be a woman and she's going to be a sister."

❖

Still Trini is at peace here in the quiet courtyard. The cruciform building, the votive figures remind her that she and the monks serve a common purpose. It's a relief not to have to explain. On their ride so far the sisters have been challenged by angry fundamentalists, accused of witchcraft, hounded by outraged civilians who hate celibates. They've battled brigands who want their laptops and their bikes and they've opened their palms to show that they mean no harm to embattled encampments of survivalists. Now they are, if not safe in the priory, at least comfortable.

Agatha has produced tea laced with mead made by the

monks, and stolid, responsible Perpetua has made a stew from their meat and the monks' vegetables. In exchange for fresh produce and a place to rest, Trini had given some salted beef and a new computer program to the abbot, who is in his quarters running it now.

The program Sister Lucy devised is not so different from the system of zero information proof, in which the operator identifies parameters to describe the center, and manages to do so without giving away any critical details. It also has certain things in common with formulae devised to leapfrog steps in any process and so speed the progress toward the infinite number. Rapt, the abbot runs Lucy's figures again and again with slight variations in an incessant attempt to address his creator. The sisters will not see him for a while; the computer can swallow you whole, body and mind and concentration.

They are quiet for the moment, sitting with empty plates.

Because it is weighing heavily, Trini finally clears her throat and says what she's been trying to say. She's surprised by how final it sounds. "It may be that we are riding in for the convergence that comes at the end of the world."

Pragmatic Perpetua snorts. "In some dinky little Arizona town?"

Trini thinks: well Bethlehem was pretty dinky, but she knows this will sound fatuous. She shrugs. "Stranger things have happened."

Perpy says bluntly, "Like what?"

Well, like her own—what was it—conversion. Trini at sixteen: ordinary Mary Alice Warner, smart and pretty and irreverent, unwitting Mary Alice Warner going along like any ordinary high school girl until she was pulled out of the air in midflight like Saul of Tarsus, twirled around and set down facing in a new and unexpected direction.

She took it hard. Cried. *Lord, I don't want to do this.*

Who would want to do this?

She tried to bargain with God. *Not me, OK?* But this God is a hard master. From the beginning she had no choice. When she accepted it, she had to break the news to people she loved even though she knew it would hurt them. Her parents were hard enough. The boy who loved her was harder. She drove Billy Deaver to the beach in her vintage Mustang to break the news to him; passionate Mary Alice Warner telling her boyfriend who would never understand, no matter how carefully she explained it. She loved him, but she loved this more.

"You're breaking us up to do this?" he cried.

"I don't even know what this is," she said.

"Son of a bitch!" He was so angry he was shouting. "You can't touch it. You can't even see it?"

"Listen, Billy. I can't even understand it."

"And you're going to throw everything away for something you don't even know what it is."

"I am." In love with a mystery. No wonder he was hurt and angry. She made her voice soft. "I'm sorry."

"Wait. Look!" Billy took her hand and spun her around. With the other hand he made a wide sweep that caught the pink sand, the light on the water, the violent sunset and brought them all back to her. "You're going to say goodbye to this?" The pressure of his fingers in the soft flesh of her palm made it clear what he was talking about. The current between them.

She hated hurting him. "I have to. It's important."

"More important than me," he said bitterly.

"More important than me," she said and then stopped

talking and hugged him hard because there were no words to explain it.

Billy said, "What about sex?"

And letting her hands slide down his arms for the last time Mary Alice Warner, who would leave behind everything—even her name—patted Billy like a beloved but outgrown plaything she had set aside for good because she was all grown up now.

She was wise enough not to tell him she had to shut off that urgent, distracting, wonderful part of her life if she was ever going to open herself to the next one.

Billy backed away. "That's crazy."

She whirled, astonished by laughter. "I know it is."

Sitting in the abbey courtyard Trini understands that she is using extreme measures to effect a transformation. The discipline, even the severe new name are all aids to this end. As Mary Alice Warner she was only a woman, designed for a limited role in the movie of life. As Trinitas, she's not there yet, but she's closer.

In transit, Trini thinks. *We are all in transit.*

Reluctantly, she gets to her feet, slapping her helmet against her boot in a gesture the others recognize. Groaning, they unfold and stand because it's clear Trini expects them to ride on tonight, stopping for prayers at midnight and unrolling sleeping bags for the few hours that stand between them and morning.

Her friend Ag grumbles, "I hope you know what you're doing."

Trini says in a low voice, "Me too." Her aim or goal—whatever it is—shimmers just out of reach, a troubling hair's breadth beyond her powers to express it. She turns to the others, who are less inclined to argue because they haven't known her as long as Ag has. She loves her colleagues because even without knowing exactly why they are riding out with her, they came without question.

They think it's important precisely because Trini does.

She dips her head in a silent prayer for them all, for the mission. Then she lifts it and slaps her helmet against the top of her boot.

"OK, let's get moving."

❖

At her fully-equipped dressing table in her lavish bedroom, surrounded by mousses, gels, moisturizers, eyeliners and eye shadow in a hundred different shades, Courtney catches the reflection of something moving. She whirls and throws a perfume bottle: "Motherfucker!"

A cat has gotten into the room somehow, although Courtney keeps her place locked even with the men gone. As she whirls, the reflection slips out of the frame, but the sliding glass doors are open just far enough to admit a large cat or a thin person. She reaches for her gun.

What's the matter here? What would she have seen if she'd turned a minute sooner? Who's out there? Armed, she pushes the doors wide and runs onto the balcony, ready to nail the crouching intruder or cut the escaping silhouette in two with a spray of bullets but if there was anybody out there he's already turned the corner. She stands there breathing hard. There's no sound but the thunder inside her own head, and except for the rush of the departing cat, no sign of movement.

A cat! She hates the things.

A cat right here in my room! The proximity leaves her

shaking.

Her first thought: Did Chag send you?

Her second: Fucking rapist.

She shouts into the dark: "Kitten Joe!"

Damn you. The only real man on Schell Isle has never even looked at her. Restless and alone, he crosshatches the island without reference to Courtney or any of the others. If she calls to get his attention he pulls the hat brim down and stalks away. It's killing her. Reflected in the eyes of all the men she's ever met, Courtney is formidable in her beauty. To the shaggy recluse she calls Kitten Joe, she is as nothing.

This is once too often, Courtney thinks angrily, even though her identification of the intruder is by no means certain.

The women may be proud of their record—no violence on Schell Isle since the Departure—but. Courtney sets her jaw. It's time to get rid of Kitten Joe forever. He is gaunt, weird. He's the only man who is indifferent to her. Mopping up the spilled perfume, Courtney would like nothing better than to collect a mob and go after Kitten Joe with torches. They ought to smoke him out, him and his seething mass of cats and set the place on fire, and if somebody else got hurt in the *melee*, for instance an arch-rival, who would know the difference?

She knows what Chag would say if she suggested burning out the intruder, but Courtney keeps her own counsel. When she explodes, which will be soon, she won't wait for permission.

❖

If she knew how much space she occupied in Courtney's

mind, Chag would be surprised.

If outside of office hours Chag thinks about Courtney at all, which is unlikely, it is as fulfilling a necessary but unpleasant function. Even in the absence of men, which has meant a virtual end to physical threats and acts of violence, it's important to maintain police as a deterrent. To theft and unwanted intrusion. To the Outlaws. To anybody else who tries to upset the established order here in the women's colony.

But Chag isn't wasting any thought on Courtney. She's turned in on herself now, touching the place in her heart that was ripped open by the Departure. She has a letter from Toby. Crumpled and grease-stained, smeared with illegible post-marks from a dozen different places, it turned up in her *In* basket this morning. How? She puts it to her face with shaking hands. Where did it come from? Is it real? Was it mailed before he was lost and declared missing or after? Can she hope or was it found and mailed by whoever found the body and went through the pockets?

What if this means he is not dead or missing after all?

What if it means he's alive and well and still out there somewhere, mailing letters?

"I miss you," says Toby's letter, perhaps from beyond the grave. "It helps to know you miss me just as much. Without you waiting, I couldn't do this at all."

What does he mean, *miss*? What does he need from her? Chag understands from the letter's tone, from the heated haste the handwriting indicates and the words for love that he lists, one after another in the text, that Toby is hard up, and for the same reasons she herself is hard up, a fact that mystifies and angers her.

In the most perfect of worlds, Chag thinks, we would be

autonomous. The trouble is that right now even... No. Almost. Almost Squiggy looks good to her.

She is aware that for some of the women on the island the Departure spelled relief from a petty annoyance—importuning in the night, the need to pretend something that disgusted or at best failed to interest them. Still others have found their own solutions, but they are not Chag's solutions. Need leaves her scattered when her life should be clearing up.

With Toby gone she had expected great feats of concentration, a void into which tough poems would rush. With him declared missing she thought with enough time and undivided concentration on the loss she might be able to write such astonishing verse that in the end it might help make up for it. Instead she is crippled by the absence. Day and night she feels it, sighs over it and uneasily scans the sky for first signs of impending doom, a desert cyclone or a single speck on the horizon—the messenger coming with news of the surrender, or the swarm—an invading enemy army.

Oh hell, she's probably looking for Toby.

Holding his letter to her cheek Chag is stirred. No. Troubled. By something she still can't put a name to.

The first intimations of the Return?

The worst thing she can imagine: the Return, all right, all those men she knows marching back

—without Toby.

As she puts down the letter a shadow slips past her window, so swift that a woman a second slower or a fraction less sharp would have missed it. Chag starts; then she relaxes. It's only Kitten Joe, with the heavy beard and the mantle of cats and the battered hat to shield his true identity. She knows nothing about him but she thinks of him as a benign presence. Even though his shadow is long gone, she raises a hand as if to salute him.

In ordinary circumstances she would draw the curtains and relax. In ordinary times she would let down; she might even let herself cry. Right now she can't. She can't even sit down.

The place is too still.

What's troubling Chag now is the apparent absence of danger. Swearing under her breath she paces and turns, turns and paces. With everything running smoothly on Schell Isle, the systems working and even the 360-degree sky clear and brilliant; with everything she needs at hand—all the comforts, talent, power, why is she so uneasy and distracted?

There is something about the sheer perfection of the surface; something about the play of sunlight on the polished woods in her serene living room; something about the absence of incident on the police department terminal in her study; there is something about the air of *peace* here that sets her jangling with anticipation.

The phrase comes to Chag whole from early American history. *Hey there, what's that sound, something big is coming 'round...*

It seems important for her to go and check on the other women.

❖

Given leave to visit her friend's bedside, Nella growls, "Eat, damn you."

"I love you," Stephanie says and tears slide down her translucent face. "I love you but I can't."

I sit here and try to make her eat, Nella thinks bitterly, shoving food in my own mouth and going, Num num while she's so sick she just smiles and doesn't swallow. I shovel it in even though the last thing I want is to get stronger. I have to keep chewing and acting like I like it just to get Steph to eat at least a little.

It isn't fair. She doesn't want to die and can't help it, and all I want is to go where she is heading.

For reasons she'd be too depressed to number and too embarrassed to discuss with you, Nella tried suicide and botched it. Can't even do this right. She remembers thinking: *This'll show him.* She almost managed, too, might have if somebody hadn't come in too soon and found her. Heroic measures. *You think I'm going to thank you?* She was out like a burned-out bulb, everything wonderfully black and she was probably sliding out of the whole ugly picture when they dragged her back to life, kicking and screaming. Set up on her two feet against her own will by first-rate doctors.

Can't even do this right she thought while they were still working her arms and legs and begging her to open her eyes to them. But semi-comatose, Nella was hiding inside her own head and she would not come out until she was good and ready.

Fuck it all, she thinks, watching Stephanie's polite smile as she turns over a piece of cake with her fork and does not pick it up. I just got hungry.

"I don't want to do this," she shouted, infuriated by her own failure.

"Back from the grave," the doctors said. They were so proud! "Your heart stopped."

"Well why didn't you just let it?"

They swelled with self-importance. "A medical miracle." "You'll get written up in all the journals." The doctors were so smug, so fixed on their accomplishments that they wouldn't hear her. It didn't matter; snatched from the arms of death, Nella was still too weak to hurt herself again. "We went to great lengths to save you."

"Why can't you just let me die."

This got their attention. "What, and make us look bad?" They put a twenty-four hour guard on her.

Now that Nella is well enough to get around, they keep the guard but they do let her visit her friend Stephanie under the mistaken impression that this will make her count her blessings. Nella is stronger than they think, but keeps this secret. When she gets strong enough she'll do it right, OK?

In spite of Stephanie's best efforts, she is dying, a fact that is disproportionately painful to Nella because so many people love Stephanie and want her to go on living: her daughters, her man. It isn't fair! Nella comes to the sickroom every day now at mealtimes because it's important to her to help keep Steph going.

At the moment, Stephanie's nurse and Nella's blowzy guard are taking advantage of this visit to grab a cigarette on the balcony. They depend on their two invalids, one physical, one spiritual, to maintain mutual surveillance.

Stephanie smiles and weakly waves the spoon away. "This seems to be good for you." She could mean Nella's visit, their manless state; she could mean anything.

Nella rocks with anxiety. "What!"

"Really. You look better. You're almost back to normal."

Normal. Nella would like to tear the flesh off her own rosy face; she'd like to strip her bones. She hates the body David got tired of. She'd do anything to keep from feeling this way. Anything. But her friend Stephanie's smile is so bright and warm that she has to say, "Thank you."

"You're getting it back," Stephanie says carefully and in a

rash moment of hope completes the thought. "If you can do it, I can. When I get better we can go shopping together. We can take a trip to Greece. Egypt. Anywhere."

Nella is staggered by the scope of this assumption. She puts her head in her hands; she can't let Stephanie see her face.

But Stephanie's presumption is even greater. Before she drifts off she says, "You have to have been where you and I have been and back again to really love life for what it is."

"Speak for yourself," Nella says. But exhausted by the simple fact of company Stephanie has lapsed, sliding down in the bed with her head bent so her neck looks cracked. If she isn't asleep, she's comatose. What Nella says next is either threat or prayer. Her heart jitters in a wild joy as she puts these words in the air between her and her sleeping friend: "Swap you."

❖

Separated by hundreds of miles, K. talks regularly to her friends M. and A. in what turns out to be the last year of their lives; although M. and A. only met once, each is hungry for news of the other.

❖

I'm going to get mine at last, Queenie Outlaw thinks. She will not know whether she means property, or vengeance. The insult and the injury are so tied up in each other that Queenie can't begin to tell you whether it's more important to reestablish her family in the dried lakebed at Schell Isle or to kill everybody and do everything to get even.

But everything is at a standstill.

Prince has spun out again.

They have to wait until his brain gets back from wherever it's traveling.

In the vacant lot outside the loft building, the Outlaws' vehicles are assembled in formation. The jumbled armory is empty now; the rusty, dangerous-looking vehicles spray-painted with the pink fist Queenie has chosen as her emblem are loaded with every conceivable kind of weapon.

The Outlaws are nothing if not inventive. For their raid on Schell Isle they have assault weapons, firebombs, grenades and homemade Molotov cocktails but they have another unexpected item in their arsenal. Each is armed with a pump gun filled with a non-lethal but disfiguring acid. Queenie's own daughters Duchess, Princess and Lady have taken instructions but privately decided not to use theirs. Her boys are more phlegmatic; pump guns will do the job, even though the results will be revolting. There are ways of killing a man that leave no trace, but none sufficient to the rage of the Outlaws' vengeful mother. Only Queenie could tell you why she's chosen the acid guns. Things that explode and things that shoot armor-plated projectiles will do for any-body who happens to stand in their way and they will be useful when they swarm the tollgate and disarm the elec-tronic barrier, but the acid has a special purpose. It is intended for the women.

"Rich bitches with their fur coats and fancy cars," Queenie says irrationally. She has a picture in her mind of what she intends to destroy. Poor and outcast as she is, bullnecked and lumbering, disfigured by zits and missing teeth, she has seen their like on television: gorgeous models with perfect bodies in expensive clothes, redolent of the gym and wrapped in money. Even naked these women would still have the flawless hair and finely-tuned bodies that she thinks come automatically with money and privilege, the porcelain complexions. They would have the money.

The hell of it is that with most of the men gone, these glowing, long-haired creatures with the sexy bodies don't just get in and out of cars or model furs for the cameras. They are mayors, police chiefs, governors. Where Queenie has strength, these walking Barbies have all the power.

Feeding on the irony, Queenie grows huge. When she was an ugly girl living in a mud hut she thumbed the magazines and watched TV and dreamed that when the right day dawned her life would improve. The zits would disappear. A dentist would fix her teeth. She'd get the right hair and by God she would be beautiful. Now she understands that nothing begets nothing.

And nothing is what she has.

What little she used to have was taken away from her.

Men did it, sure.

But she blames the women.

Well she'll show them. With the help of her clan, Queenie is going to storm Schell Isle and bring these women down. With the men gone, the women have gotten soft.

Like, did they bother to ride out when Earl dropped the fetish on them?

They've let down their guard; with nothing going on and no trouble expected until the men come back, they've been lulled into the illusion of safety. Queenie has seen it in their faces on the TV; she's caught the listless, inattentive edge to the acting governor's orders.

Although she hates all privileged women everywhere, Queenie has focused on Schell Isle for two reasons. It is where she personally started out—the only place she had. And it's overrun by the handsome rich, who had more than Queenie does even when they woke up naked on the morning of the first day.

Schell Isle is isolated, easily encompassed. The perfect target. Let the beautiful women be ruined.

Let Queenie spring up to take their place.

She thinks of herself as legion.

Once she's entrenched, no power on earth can remove her.

Queenie thinks, not for the first time, *Serve them right.* And laughs so hard all the kids can see the cavities in her molars.

After she and her wonderful brood have cut the cable and knocked out the electronic barrier, after they've neutralized everybody on the island with the gas she has lashed to the back of the Outlaw trucks in metal canisters, she is going to have the stupefied women dragged into the square. First off, she's going to wake them up and let her tough, strong, angry boys have their way with them, a payback for a lifetime of loyalty in dark places. Queenie saw the way women of Schell Isle looked at her boys back in the old days. *Lower than...*

She snorts. "Who do you think you are, assholes?"

What with the war and physical ruin compounded by the exigencies of life in the underclass in a hostile city, Earl, Prince and Lord, Count and Baron haven't had more than a couple of women between them since the troubles.

Yes, Queenie will have the glossy bitches dragged into the square and she'll let her boys have their way with them, and when that's done she'll have them shave the women's heads and singe their scalps to so no more hair will ever grow there, and in case these babes have wigs at home she will use the acid to permanently rearrange all those pretty faces. What's more they will take pictures. Close up and in color. Videotape for CNN.

Next to them she will look good, and knows it.

At some point in her life Queenie was given Thorazine, which made her grind her remaining teeth so hard they shattered into jagged points. She feels the colliding rows of teeth grating. *The fairest in the land*, she thinks.

"Oh Mama," Princess says anxiously, touching Queenie's arm. It is almost as if she's heard Queenie thinking. "We're not going to hurt these people, are we?" Princess is pregnant. Motherhood has made her soft.

Queenie sticks a billy club into her creaking leather belt and answers her daughter with a short, ugly laugh. "Oh hell no, honey. We're just going to mess them up a little bit."

In the far corner of the lot where the vehicles are assembled, towheaded Prince stands apart. It doesn't matter what happens or who tries to speak to him; he's gone someplace that they can't travel. Solitary, gripped, he just whirls and whirls, with jutting teeth and windmilling arms. Prince spins with his hair standing out like the petals on a blown chrysanthemum and his green eyes empty of everything but the vision.

He's been like this for three days.

Queenie's breath catches. *What, son? What is it?*

His irises are huge and spinning; *I don't know!*

Perhaps because she is thinking for two now, Princess tugs her mother's arm. "Mama, mama, what's the matter with Prince?"

"Don't pay him no never mind," Queenie says quickly because it is important not to know what the fates may be trying to tell her. She is about to leave with Earl to get the nerve gas. At the bottom of her black heart is a gash from which rage bubbles.

82

In spite of what she tells her kids, it's not the eviction from Schell Isle that festers at the bottom of Queenie's heart and fuels her hatred of the women. It is the worst betrayal of all, the one she's never told anyone. She is riding out because even in the early days her very own *King* made love to her with his eyes squinched shut. He couldn't stand to look at her.

In the kingdom of the blind, she would be gorgeous.

Who wouldn't want to load up and ride across the desert and onto Schell Isle where the handsome, heartless women live? Who wouldn't want to pay them all back for the insult of comparisons?

❖

Courtney strides into Chag's office and dumps the thing on her blotter. It is ugly and dark with blood. "Look at this. This is one thing too many," she shouts.

Again—once again!—Chag puts aside the poem she's been grappling with. It's hard to say exactly what the bloody, blackened thing Courtney has dropped really is: another fetish? Part of a corpse? It could be anything: a lump of radioactive matter, a botched head-shrinking job. In fact it appears to be at least partly made up of dead cat. "Where did you find it?"

"That's not important," Courtney says shortly. "Something's coming down, OK? We've got to act. Ream out incursions, fortify the place. Move all the rolling stock into the lakebed and plant more gun emplacements. Arm this fucking place."

"Against what?"

"You know." With a wave of her hand she indicates the

entire world. "Everything that's out there."

What is Courtney expecting? It's not clear. Who does she want to kill? *Everyone*, Chag thinks. *Me*. Temperate Chag says, "Be cool. Nothing's happened yet."

Courtney slaps the object on the desk. "What do you call this!"

The thing on Chag's desk could be something Courtney has made to stampede her. "You don't even know what that is," Chag says.

"Hell yes I do. It's the final straw." Courtney's black hair is like a stormcloud around her creamy face. She puts both fists on Chag's desk and leans hard. "It's the men. We've got to get rid of them."

"They've been gone for years!"

Courtney doesn't hear. "They're all the same. That fucking hermit. Him and those spooky, spooky cats. Let's burn the fucker out. And Squiggy. Squiggy's got to go."

Kitten Joe. What does Courtney have against him? It is a mystery. Urgency makes Chag's voice sharp. "No!" For the second time in the course of these interviews, she takes her gun out of the desk. "You're under orders not to touch anybody."

"What, you're just going to let them roll over us?"

"There isn't any *them*, Court." Uneasily, Chag adds, "At least, not yet."

"You know what happens if you let down."

"You have your orders."

"Anything can happen to you." Courtney is trembling with fury. Her voice clots with the possibilities. "Get it? Anything."

Chag stands. "Orders!"

"This is only the beginning," Courtney shouts. Beautiful

Courtney does not always use pretty words. "You want us to get caught sitting around with our thumbs up our asses? Permission requested."

Let Courtney begin and I have unleashed the whirlwind. "Permission refused."

"Then I'll just…"

"You'll just nothing." Coming around the desk Chag grips Courtney's wrists, digging her fingers in. "Not without my sayso." Then she releases her police chief and sits down. She fixes on her terminal and does not look up again until she hears Courtney slam the door.

Keep the faith, she writes. A first line has just delivered itself to her.

It comes so naturally! *If you must, dissemble.*

She has it. She has the opening lines of the unwritten *Road Kills.*

Keep the faith.

If you must, dissemble.

Chag draws a jagged breath because she does not know what the next line means; rather, she hears the voice clearly but cannot say where it's coming from. It leaves her feeling expectant, somehow unfinished. She will be like a knight circling the globe with half a talisman, looking for the person who holds the other half:

Look upon my face and tremble.

❖

Q. Name two organizing principles. A. Theology and narrative. The first is an attempt to define or justify our relationship to the eternal. The second, an attempt to order what happens to us.

85

✤

What Trini hopes for, riding into Arizona: She does not know. She thinks it might be kind of neat—even glorious— if the world really did turn out to be about to end.

And she and the Little Sisters of the Apocalypse are summoned to be present.

Like most of us Trini would prefer a final resolution, some definite, conclusive event that might let her go out on a high note. In grammar school the nuns had taught her that martyrs went directly to heaven. This might not be such a bad thing. Better instant death in the name of God than living too long and getting old and demoralized. She doesn't want to end up failing everybody and losing everything and traducing or betraying her own hopes in the long, deteriorating slide into a messy old age and an ugly death.

Death for a cause is probably too much to hope for, but she thinks about it. She does.

For the moment, however, Trini has to be content with the fact that she and the others are headed for a place where they will be needed.

In the past they've ridden in to exterminate viruses in civil and religious computer systems, to rescue communities from terrorists, to surprise assassins in the act, to bring medicine to the sick and food to the hungry and in at least one case to prevent a suicide, but this time? What the sisters have to do on Schell Isle is not yet clear, although Trini is certain that in due time it will be revealed. Right now it's enough to be on the way.

She understands that it is important to believe in what you're doing.

Reverse the coin; it is important to be doing something

you believe in. It is purpose, not product that we value.

Thus Trini, riding into the Arizona night to effect a rescue; Trini, who has shed the last silly vestiges of sweet young Mary Alice Warner to become tough, driven Sister Trinitas of the Little Sisters of the Apocalypse; Trini, in mid-transformation.

❖

Who are the sisters riding in to rescue anyway?

The women, one assumes, but as a group? If not as a group, then which of the women are they coming to snatch from the jaws of death here, and is it death by her own hand or death by disease or assassination or natural disaster? Or will the Little Sisters of the Apocalypse be called to pull her out of some dreadful hand-to-hand battle with an adversary yet to be identified?

What are they riding in to save the women from?

Is the danger approaching from outside?

Or is the enemy within?

Is it the Outlaws who are the threat here or is it Kitten Joe who's the menace, or will it be lascivious, greasy-fingered Squiggy, who works for the women by day and by night skulks in ditches outside the lighted windows of their houses? Or is it Courtney's anger that is the true enemy, or the destructive power of Verena's grief? Is it the threat of the disease that wastes Stephanie or is it the spirit that grips Nella and smothers her in a romantic, incomplete embrace with death? Maybe it's Squiggy who is the ultimate enemy, defecating in Sarah's silver drawer as she says goodbye to the last of her business breakfast guests; or it could be the Outlaw family, fully girded and prepared at last and fueling their ragtag collection of industrial and army surplus vehicles, packing the last few things they'll need for their long-awaited move on Schell Isle.

Or the Little Sisters of the Apocalypse may be riding out to protect Schell Isle from some unexpected freak of nature, an earthquake that could engulf the island, or a storm so sudden and violent that nobody can prepare for it.

The long-awaited nuclear holocaust.

Attack by wild beasts.

Panic in the night.

The astounding tidal wave.

The end of the world.

The return of the men.

There is the possibility that it is in fact the missing men who pose the threat here, mates and lovers who have been absent for so long that some people assume they're gone for good. Kiss him goodbye, miss him terribly and waste your days waiting for him to come back and then go about your lives. When you next look up it will be with this perception.

When he comes back he'll be changed.

When he comes back everything will change.

Your worst nightmare. Your heart's desire. It may be this that discovers the women snapping to attention in the middle of the night and sets them revolving, barefoot, through their empty rooms and it may be this that gives them the dry swallows and leaves them gulping in combined despair and desire while on the last leg of their motorized cavalry charge through the Arizona desert the Little Sisters of the Apocalypse ride on in the first flush of gallantry that is anticipated but as yet unfocused.

❖

K.'s mother was a widow for fifty years.

❖

In the dried out and cracked lakebed the skeletons of fish stir and spring upright as if the desiccated owners are dancing on their tails. The dry air begins to move before a desert breeze and like Chag, the other women find themselves shifting, whirling in the extraordinary isolation of three a.m., going— one more time—to look out each of their windows; it would appear that after years filled with waiting, something is about to happen.

Soon.

It's humming in the desert air.

Soon.

Impatient, frazzled and distracted, the sleepless Chag says into the night: "Whoever you are, hurry."

5

*A teaching nun and a poet, K.'s first mentor was allowed to spend
six months in a Carmelite convent. The rule: silence, prayer before
dawn, work, a routine of prayer, sacrifice and contemplation. Food
was plain, scant. At Christmas and Easter, to celebrate the feast,
each nun had five M&Ms counted into her hand.*

The Little Sisters of the Apocalypse were founded as a
cloistered order; what was it they called themselves? A
powerhouse of prayer. Locked in silence, the dedicated
contemplatives would storm heaven. When the new Mother
Superior was named in Trini's first year, she looked around
at the Nineties and decided more was needed. The sisters
were released to take classes at the university; with a gift from
an anonymous donor, the Superior bought three computer
terminals and had them wired to the university mainframe.
A few: Trini, Lucy, loyal Agatha and even crusty Perpetua
were quick to learn. Running figures in an attempt to divine
the nature of eternity, the sisters hoped to develop a surer
way. If they could quantify the goal and identify stages, or
steps, they just might define the approach to eternity.

Learning, the sisters wrote two new languages and developed several utilities to market, bringing in money to keep the order going and to feed the poor.

Pressing operating systems to the limit in their attempt to map infinity, the sisters always seemed close. But close is not *there*. Close is nowhere.

This is why Trini leans into the wind and pushes her bike faster, faster, gunning her motors for the leap into eternity.

When the university's old mainframe was donated to the sisters and installed in the cloister, five reactionary nuns offended by the apparent violation of the vow of silence barricaded themselves in the chapel. They declared a hunger strike, to last until the Mother Superior stepped down and the old order was restored. It was clear, however, that even for reactionaries, the Nineties had arrived. Before they clumped in and barricaded the door with heaped *prie-dieux*, the recalcitrant sisters passed a note to a junior sister who called the media.

Reporters came. Photographers came. TV news cameras came along with *Hard Copy* and *Current Affair*, but they were restricted to the convent courtyard where nothing was going on and had to satisfy themselves with terse sound bites from the Mother Superior.

Trini will never forget the siege in the chapel, reporters and photographers clumped outside in silence, waiting for answers to questions they'd written down and slipped through a crack in the tightly locked doors. She has by heart the curt written responses.

Understand us, the entombed sisters wrote.

Understand me, the Superior wrote them in a note slipped through the crack.

"We are both trying to do the same things," she told Trini.

"And look. We are at cross purposes."

No two ways to heaven are the same, Trini realizes.

What we had was good, the next note said.

And the Superior wrote: *Things aren't necessarily good just because they're old.*

But even as she did so the old woman mourned for gentler days when the Rule was spelled out in black and white, when shades of grey were never imagined. Everything was cut and dried. You knew what was expected. Proceeding by the numbers was much less taxing than the relentless pressure and continually changing circumstances that come with regular examination of conscience. If she grieved for the absolutism of the past, the Superior turned with gratitude to the fresh possibilities opened by the present. How to explain this to a group of reactionary nuns committed to living the life of the medieval church to the exclusion of the contemporary one?

The Superior wrote to the entombed sisters: *if everything that rises must converge, we must use everything that's given us in an attempt to start rising.*

This note slipped through the crack in the bolted doors that shut out the grieving Superior was the last. It was never answered.

Out of respect, Mother refused to let the SWAT team in to flush out the protesters. Although the recalcitrants never showed themselves, supplies left outside the bolted doors by night were always gone in the morning. As days stretched into months the police and the press got bored and went away and in the end, the embattled sisters died in the chapel. Nobody was quite sure how. The chaplain celebrated a Mass of the Resurrection outside the doors right before Mother had the place bricked up and plaqued so that into the next millennium, outsiders would know what had happened here. Grieved but prayerful, the Little Sisters of the Apocalypse moved into the present, hoping for the future. Mother died of heart failure within the year and Trini was named Superior.

We are all trying to do the same things, Trini thinks, fearful and exalted, and with a lift of the heart she comes over the last rise and looks down at the tollgate and the warning signs that protect Schell Isle, the causeway beyond. She brings her bike to an abrupt stop and waits with one booted foot planted firmly in the white sand until the others are all ranged on the ridge beside her.

And now here we are.

Trini's heart turns over. She can hear her breath rattling around in her helmet. They are at the brink of the dry lake that surrounds the island.

❖

In the shack on the far side of the island cats stir and swarm around Kitten Joe's feet, puddling on the floor around his chair. Kneading the raw wood of the floor with sheathed paws, they flex their bodies. Even though they're too far away to see or hear what's happening at the tollbooth on the far side of the causeway, the animals jump on the recluse's lap and perch on his shoulders. His head lifts.

Everything in him rushes toward a moment of convergence. His voice creaks as if his throat has rusted from disuse. "Who calls?"

❖

"Shit. Fuck. Shit!"

Who's speaking? It could be Courtney. It could be Squiggy, looking up from whatever he's just been doing with bloody hands and a bloody mouth.

❖

Forgive Verena, it's all she's ever been able to think about. She's spent her life fixed on the Return, and if it's not this Return? Her voice pipes as sweetly as it did when she was five years old. "Daddy?"

❖

The air is humming; Chag does not so much hear as sense it. Leaving her office she walks, blinking, into the dazzling, still morning. *Oh my God, it's today.*

❖

"Shit, oh shit," Courtney growls. Something is coming. "It's too soon." Separated from her equipment as she is, planting land mines on the point on the far side of the island, she does not so much hear as comprehend the thrum of motors: someone approaching.

Is it the Return? Is it? Flat on her belly in the tall, thin grass on the far side of the island, she feels her pelvis twisting in a sharp, involuntary thrust. Men. When they're here, Courtney has to have them all. She's trying to annihilate them. Or herself. Have men, have them all and keep having them; have enough men for long enough in your slippery, sad life and their faces will blur. You can make them disappear, she thinks. *Or I will.*

94

Courtney used to have her men in such quick succession that they blurred and melted away, running in a puddle like Little Black Sambo's circling tigers. She would do this and do it and still rise in the morning with the smile of a fresh virgin.

Too many was the same as none. This is how she erased them.

Shit! She realizes now that for all this she can never erase the scorn of her father. It hangs on a hook in the front of Courtney's mind like a filthy rag; it blackens her soul:

We wanted a boy.

Bastard, bastard. Erase them all.

Sure she wants to kill her father.

Even after Robert made his hurt speech about the pressure of her expectations, her departing lover dragged his hands down her arms as if fate was tearing him away against his will. "I love you. I'm doing this for you. I hate leaving you." He didn't sound sorry, he sounded glad. "I'll be back." Sensing her resentment he added, "I'm going to make you proud of me."

Today Courtney snarls, "Don't do me any favors."

❖

Life goes on in the same old way at the Outlaws' hideout. Everything's in readiness. They've been ready for days but frustrated as she is by the holdup, Queenie has not been able to give her troops their marching orders.

"Typical," she grumbles. She is sitting on the steps outside the door to the loft building in full battle gear: leather pants, tough boots, assault weapon and belt with extra clips, the last Desert Storm jacket in captivity. Her earrings are cascading silver grenades; she is beyond ready and yet, fully armed and hot to go, she knows they are stalled here. "Fucking typical."

Unlike the expedient islanders, whose polite society organizes them and dictates their marching orders, Queenie and her kin are rebels. They don't march to a different drummer.

They don't march to any drummer.

They march when they feel like it.

At the moment Queenie is the only one who feels like it.

The others are upstairs sprawling with their mates or drowsing in the shade of their vehicles in the ruined parking lots. If Queenie goes among them kicking them to attention, they yawn and mumble, "Yes, Ma." "Sure Queens, sure-sure," indicating willingness, but even the outsiders who've become members of the Outlaw clan know as well as Queenie does that there's nothing anybody can do about moving out until the last member of the group is good and ready. And the holdup? Yes there is a holdup.

Prince. He's Queenie's favorite, her fairest, her most beautiful. In that preternatural bonding of mothers and special sons that transcends words, Prince has let her know that he is not ready.

Right now he's out in the road in front of the place leaning against the hood of his Jeep, perfectly relaxed but with his head tilted at a peculiarly twisted angle, so that he seems to be staring at something over his right shoulder where as far as Queenie can tell, there is only a dead tree.

"Oh shit," she says. "Shit shit. What do you see, baby?"

She hopes to God he doesn't think he sees a person perched in its branches. She hopes he isn't waiting for it to speak to him.

❖

The Little Sisters of the Apocalypse seem to be stalled at the tollgate on the mainland. Standing outside the hermetically sealed tollgate, they maintain their formidable, neatly organized wedge, sixteen black-leather clad figures in helmets with the silver crosses glinting in the sun. Straddling their bikes, they're still waiting for Trini to give the go-ahead.

Behind the layers of bulletproof plexi, the guard studies them. Friends or foes? She doesn't know. All she knows is that whatever comes down here, she's not going to be made responsible. She's not about to give the bikers entry on her own hook. The orders have to come from higher up. Somehow reassured by the leader's manners, the uniformity of the silver emblems on the helmets, she's passed on Trini's message. She's going to make damn good and sure she has official approval from Chag before she even considers it.

Their query comes up on the screen in Chag's office, phrased by Trini but entered by good Myrna, who does more shifts than any of the other women who stand guard there. Chag taps out a quick response and as quickly makes voice contact.

"Myrna. This is Chag. What do you have?"

"I... I'm not sure. Somebody wants to come aboard here. It's a kind of a—a kind of a delegation." The guard's breath whistles in the mouthpiece.

Thank God, Chag thinks. After five years of the monotony of solitude, she's starved for change. At last something new is happening. Still she is responsible for the wellbeing of the women here so she has to proceed carefully. She has to ask, "Hostiles?"

"I don't think so," Myrna says. "They look OK."

"Armed?"

"Not that I can see."

Chag's heart lifts; still she has to be cautious. She must ask all the right questions. "How many?"

"Sixteen."

"Not more than we can handle. Sex?"

"Women, I think." Myrna looks at the bikers but she can't be sure because of the sunlight glinting off their faceplates. The leader is slight; as a group they are shorter than a group of men, but that isn't the real difference. The difference is in attitude. Instead of trying to argue their way in, they wait for her to get back to them. "Shall I send them away?"

"Not yet. No. I don't think so."

The bikers' group image blurs in the heat. The group seems to hang in place, shimmering as if just about to explode into movement. Still they are waiting for Myrna, who says to them, to Chag, "What do you want me to do?"

❖

Halted on the sandy shore of the dry lake, the sisters can see the island tempo accelerating. Dots that represent people mass on the far shore; cars go back and forth. Still nothing is decided. Trini has spoken to the women in the sealed booth. Messages are going back and forth. On either side of the booth they can see flecks of sand exploding into the sparks as the breeze spins them into the base of the electronic barrier. At waist height insects fly into the barrier and incinerate and far above their heads something big bursts into flames as a bird collides with the barrier and hurtles to earth like a burning fighter plane.

Exhausted by the trip, the Little Sisters of the Apocalypse stand by their bikes like young explorers halted at the gates of a forbidden city, scared and excited, anxious and eager, waiting to be admitted to the island.

❖

In life as in all narrative, there is a time when the sequence of events dictates the next thing. Whatever follows is preceded by the hesitation: the split-second spring at the end of the diving board that lets the diver know it is time. NOW.

❖

Everything changes.

Something is coming. No. It's here.

A shadow falls across the grass where Courtney is planting land mines, unaware of the crisis at the tollgate. In another minute the dubious Myrna will call her on her cellular phone. Courtney cries, "Who's there?"

Without being told she knows somebody is about to breach the security of the island, but hatred pushes her to the wrong conclusions. It comes to her whole.

Fuckers. They're trying to come back.

At a rustle in the grass she cries sharply, "Robert, you bastard. Is that you?"

Courtney is trembling, on the cusp of a decision.

"Not yet! You can't fucking come yet." She isn't ready. She thinks she does not want the men to come back at all. No. That isn't it. At last she understands.

She does want them back.

She wants them to come back so she can destroy them.

She says, apparently to nothing, "Give me a minute here!" She means, let me finish planting my mines, double the guard, get my people together. Give me time to clean out the

99

armory and empty the knife racks in every kitchen; I need all our gelignite, *plastifier*, fucking TNT; *I want enough arms to blow them to oblivion.*

In her own way vindictive Courtney is like the mad Captain Bligh, stalking the decks of the *Bounty*, slapping her thigh as she barks, *Repel all boarders.*

Courtney pulls her phone out of her belt, intending to sound the alert—too late. A shadow has fallen across her; there is a greasy hand over her mouth and the phone's gone, thrown into the sand and ground into silence. *Rape*, she thinks. *Squiggy, are you going to fucking rape me?* Struggling, she wheels, trying to confront her attacker, and crashes into the blunt instrument as it completes its arc in the air and lands with a smack, silencing her.

❖

Narrative inevitability: K. thinks for much longer than her mother does that there may be something she can do to make her get better.

❖

Reckless Chag; no telling who's out there. It could just as easily be the Outlaw family approaching in disguise, vengeful Queenie and her savage girls confecting sweet faces to make Myrna OK them. Although the exiled family is the stated reason for maintaining a police force and keeping the island armed, nobody on Chag's staff knows what the Outlaws actually look like. They were gone from Schell Isle long before the men moved their women here. So there is the possibility that the people at the gate are Outlaws in disguise. Let Myrna open the gate to Queenie and her girls and Chag will pay. Let down your guard and the Outlaw men will spring out from wherever they're hiding, swarming in like the Mongol hordes, Huns or Vandals to change the face of this little civilization.

Still!

Myrna is saying, "We don't know what we're getting into here."

"We can't spend our lives being afraid," Chag says.

"Maybe I should call Courtney for backup."

"If you want to," Chag says.

She waits with a strange detachment while Myrna tries and fails to reach the volatile second in command. It's as if she already knows what is going to be the outcome here.

Keep the faith, Chag's new poem goes. It keeps coming back on her, broaching the surface like a leaping fish; it is disturbing. *If you must, dissemble.*

Myrna says unhappily, "I can't raise her."

"Don't worry. This is my responsibility."

"What are we going to do?"

Chag hesitates.

There is a time in every narrative—as in life—that the confluence of events dictates the next thing. We don't know what we have to do, only that something deep tells us we have to do it. A momentary hesitation indicates what must come next. The silence that opens so the right words can fall into it. They come to her whole. They are on Chag's lips almost before she hears them.

It's time.

"It's time." Chag is surprised to find that excitement makes it hard to breathe.

"Are you sure? Are you really OK with this?"

"Let them pass."

"But you don't know who…"

"I do," Chag says, although this is not precisely true. And although the rest is not precisely true either, except in the metaphysical sense, Chag says firmly "I sent for them."

But as Chag and her gatekeeper deliberate, Trini raises her arm and waves her group down the bank toward the dry lakebed. Yes she sees the warning signs—the electronic barrier—but her faith precedes her. In ordinary circumstance they'd be stopped cold and nuked to cinders by the electronic barrier, but these are not ordinary people. The gatekeeper broadcasts a warning to the bikers as they roar down on the barrier and as she does so Myrna is moved as if by a huge hand, sent staggering backward into the lever that disarms the barrier.

❖

K.s mother loses the ability to speak. She's locked so deep inside it's hard to know whether she's still in there.

❖

In the middle of the empty road in front of the Outlaws' loft building, Prince goes rigid. His feet are spread; his knees lock and his arms fly out with a snap so he looks for a second like a crudely made star.

From her post on the front step Queenie watches him. "Oh fuck," she says to Earl, "I hope he hasn't fell out even farther."

He's usually gone for days, locked inside whatever the fuck he thinks he's looking at. Unless Prince is cut loose and hurtling away from her, traveling through star-shot, velvety skies to some weird, glamorous universe that Queenie would kill to reach—if only she could see where he is right now.

Then his body relaxes and takes on human contours.

Earl's breath comes out in a rush. "Wuow."

Prince blinks.

Standing, Queenie reaches for the bosun's pipe she keeps at her belt. What happens next depends on Prince. If the signs are right she'll blow the bosun's pipe and bring everyone swarming.

She waits. Prince rubs his eyes and tests his limbs one at a time.

Then he turns to his mother, looking not so much bemused as puzzled. When he sees her looking he grins.

"Let's roll," Queenie says.

Shit! His eyes click wide and his arms snap straight out from his sides and he's gone again.

Earl shouts, "What's the matter? What the fuck is the matter?"

Queenie, baffled, horrified: "Shit! The son of a bitch fell back out."

6

We are in the sandy courtyard at the center of Schell Isle: the circular, white-graveled Zen garden surrounds a fountain conceived as a monument to peace. Gouts of water circle yet another Eternal Flame. The women could not tell you what the Eternal Flame commemorates; it's one more of the men's empty gestures to peace.

Chag, Verena and Sarah have formed up in front of the fountain to greet the Little Sisters of the Apocalypse. At a signal from Trini, the sisters shed their helmets and stand bareheaded and unarmed in the brilliant sunlight. Their upturned palms let the women know the sisters mean them no harm. The nuns have pulled their motorcycles into a half-circle so that, essentially, they surround the women of Schell Isle. Because the sun is almost directly overhead, black shadows pool at their feet and under their bikes.

"Who are you?" Chag asks.

Trini is about to speak when someone cuts in.

"You know who these babes are." Raging because she is too late to prevent this incursion, Courtney strides into the square, holding a scarf to her bloody temple. "They're sickos. *Nuns!*" She spits it out like: *eunuchs.*

Ag murmurs, "Why do you hate us so much?"

Courtney does not moderate her voice. She yells. "Because you hit me." It isn't true. Also, it isn't why she hates them.

Rosy, goodnatured and tough, Perpy snorts. "Because she knows we can do without men."

But it is Trini who has the true answer. She turns to Courtney saying mildly, "We can't help it if we remind you of last things."

"I'm Charlotte Hagen," Chag says to Trini, "You are…"

Courtney snarls, "Dried up old virgins."

"I'm Sister Trinitas." Trini thinks it politic to spare the women of Schell Isle the splendor and terror of the full name. "We are the Little Sisters."

But from somewhere just out of sight a rusty voice supplies the rest of the title. Startled by speech, somebody says, "The Little Sisters of the Apocalypse."

Who? There's something familiar about the… Chag whirls, thinking to identify the speaker. *Kitten Joe?* How could it be? He doesn't come into the town center; as far as she knows he can't speak. It's weird. A bunch of strange women ride in from another world and somebody here knows them, what's the… "Who!"

A trail of shadow boils at the heels of the solitary's tall, receding shape. Taking advantage of the distraction, Courtney muscles her way into the delegation of Schell Islanders. "Fucking nuns."

Surprised by rage, Chag turns on her. "What's the big deal? "

"Just watch out for them."

"They're only women, Court."

Verena says in that little-girl voice, "Women like us."

"Not like us. No way," Courtney says bitterly. She means:

the nuns don't have her problems, not any of them. Don't care about their looks, do fine without men. So pissed she spits, "Black crows. Fucking vultures."

"What?" Even Trini is surprised.

"Turn up when something is about to die."

Something. Trini shudders. *About to die. The world?* Wary of her sworn adversary, she addresses Chag. "We're here to help you."

Courtney shows her teeth. "What for? What did you really come here for?"

Trini turns mild eyes on her. "Everything's to a purpose." She believes this: everyone is put here for a purpose. She has spent her life up until now trying to divine hers.

"Bad news," Courtney grumbles. "These women are bad news."

Chag ignores this. "Tell me why you've come."

"I can't explain exactly. I…" Trini is so filled with the compulsion and the mystery of it that the words back up, jamming her throat so she can hardly speak. At last it comes. "We're facilitators."

Chag hears a click, as if of tumblers falling into place. "I think we've been expecting you."

Ag turns to her in surprise, "We came all this way because you sent for us?"

Chag shakes her head. "I don't think so." But. ROAD KILLS! Something about… *Look upon my face and tremble.* Her unfinished poem. There's more shimmering just beyond her grasp. Weird, in this time of extreme change, Chag thinks, to be dogged by unbidden rhymes as she is, hung up a scrap of unfinished verse. Puzzled, she shakes her head. "I don't think I sent for you. What about you, Court?" She shoots her a look. "Did you?"

Courtney inflates; she's too angry to speak.

An answer falls into the silence.

It comes from Perpy. "We go where we're needed."

Instead of focusing on the transaction at hand Trini has been listening, whether for clarification or further instructions or simply a kind word she cannot say. Now she clears her throat and when they are all looking she says, "Something. Somebody. Ah."

She tries again. "Somebody told us there's going to be trouble here."

"It's those fucking Outlaws. I told you we had to arm."

"Trouble!" Chag considers. "Do you think we have enemies?"

"Everybody has enemies," Courtney says. "These women here..."

"Be quiet, Court. Sister?"

Trini says, "I don't know." She may be astounded by what she says next but as she speaks Trini realizes that she has in fact been preparing for this exact encounter, perfecting a computer program that came to her like a long dream. Unlike the eternity programs, this one spelled itself out neatly in analog units for her while they were on the road; she fine-tuned it on her laptop while the others slept. Now she understands what she's been doing and why. She says with certainty, "But I do know why we're here right now."

Even as she frames the next sentence, Trini understands that it isn't the whole reason. It may not even be the real reason. "We..."

Courtney interrupts. "You're here to fuck us up." She raises her voice for the women who have been assembling at the periphery. "These fucking nuns. They're here to fuck us up."

"Court!"

Trini says firmly, "We've brought a computer program to augment your security systems. Advanced surveillance and reporting capacity."

At this news, even Courtney brightens.

Chag says, "Everything's quiet here. I'm not sure we need..."

Trini's look silences her. "You may not need it now." Perhaps because they sense some—what, *likeness*: shared aims, both women want this encounter to go well. She finishes, "But you will."

Verena knows a little bit about this religious order: with enough time and the right number of megabytes they can accomplish anything. Find her father, lost in an old war? She puts her hand to her throat. Then she says to Chag, "Charlotte, she may be right."

"I suppose we do have enemies." The Outlaws, Chag thinks wearily. They want to make us pay for what the men did to them. To her embarrassment she isn't clear exactly what that was. *Don't they know we had nothing to do with it?* Unless. She founders on this thought: *guilt by complicity.* "I suppose we have to be ready."

"Then let's get started."

She touches Trini's arm. "What do you want in return?"

"To stay as long as it takes to install it," Trini says. "We need to get it up and running before we think about what's next." She's talking about the security program, but in her mind there is the prayer wheel containing a billion names for God and it is spinning so fast she cannot read it. She knows the means are here. Next to the sisters' klunky computers, the Schell Isle mainframe is swift as a flight of archangels; she can hardly wait to log in.

108

There are truths Trini ought to be telling these island women, things she ought to be doing, but what? With an effort she manages to keep from making the Sign of the Cross over them.

Chag says, "You can keep your motorcycles in the municipal garage. If you'd like, I'll have rooms made up for you in the lodge."

Trini says, "We'll sleep with the computers." Only she knows that there is more than one level of meaning to what she says next. That she has something to do here is clear. That she doesn't yet know what it is, is troubling. She says uncertainly, "We have to stay until the job is done."

With the sisters on the island, things change. The religious mean different things to different people: promise, menace, affront. Some of the women are drawn to them. Fascinated by their discipline, the sexual autonomy, the women of Schell Isle drift close and linger with their lips trembling with unbidden confessions. Others dodge into doorways so they won't have to speak, or glare suspiciously from windows as the motorcycles pass.

• Even the approaching Outlaws have gotten wind of the arrival. They have pulled into a deserted pueblo to regroup, trucks, vans and armored vehicles parked at the bottom of a canyon while Queenie and her people collect their thoughts. This may be a good thing, Queenie thinks. Let these weird nuns create the necessary diversion. While those rich babes she hates are distracted by these God freaks the Outlaws will swarm down on them like the wolf upon the fold. Friend or foe, those prissy nuns will be sorry they ever poked their noses out of the cloister.

• Slouching from one job to the next, Squiggy shrinks into shadows, walleyed with hatred, whenever one of the motorcycles goes by. He is not sure quite why he hates the nuns so much, only that he does. It's all right, he thinks, and feels the warm hand of lust twisting his entrails. Sooner or later he will get one of them alone and show them who is who and what's what.

• Because she's certain that these nuns are only the precursors, the first wave of the invasion she's spent her time here preparing for, Courtney is in a frenzy of preparation. Perhaps because it's the thing she's most afraid of, she decides these plainfaced women in their spooky black clothes have got to be some kind of advance team, tightly in league with the men.

Isn't it Catholics who believe women are supposed to be having babies all the time, and aren't you supposed to pop one a year until motherhood drops you and you fall over dead? These plainfaced women who don't give a fuck about their looks are scheming to bring the men back so everybody can be scared of getting pregnant all over again. They'll strip Courtney of her powers and make her drop babies like a ball gum machine. They'll make sure she loses every thing, starting with her job.

Her father's face: *We wanted a boy*. He knew. No way.

Use these nuns, Courtney thinks, you need their expertise until they get this fortification program in place. Then. She pulls her hand across her neck in a throat-cutting gesture. *Schltttt!*

The nuns' arrival has demonstrated that Courtney's sadly unprepared. She is grateful to them for alerting her to the seriousness of her situation. She's been on the phone ever

110

since they hit the island, ordering armed cars, explosives, extra weapons. When the real enemy comes, she will be ready.

• Although she is not admitted, Verena lingers in the hall outside the municipal computer lab. She has a boon to beg. The round-faced sister they call Perpetua looks friendliest; she will confront her with this problem. Because these women are not civilians but religious, Verena will couch her request in biblical terms. All she has to do is remind Perpy of the one lost sheep. *My father was lost in the war. Can you find him for me?*

• To his astonishment Kitten Joe discovers that since the nuns came, he's lost interest in his cats. The animals seem to sense this and they puddle around his feet, awaiting instructions. Mrrr-ing, they rub against his shins. The recluse isn't sure what the nuns are doing here—indeed, he doesn't know what he's doing here, only that he fetched up on the island in such a state of psychic exhaustion that until now, he hasn't given it much thought.

Paralyzed by grief without knowing what he'd lost.

He came to earth in this shack.

Cats came. They blanketed him and spoke to him and they did not so much diffuse his pain as distract him from it. It may be why he's survived. But now the solitude galls, and the cats trouble him. The changing faces of the Schell Islanders trouble him and something about the Little Sisters troubles him.

Nothing troubles him so much as the uneasy sense that until the disturbances began—the subsonic hum or whatever it is, the stirring in the air that presaged their arrival, he was essentially fixed in space, without a plan.

Then, ranging the deserted parts of the island with his cats he became aware of lights in windows at odd hours, women disrupted by something they could not identify. *Something...* The rush of change. *Is happening.* And for the first time he understood that he'd fetched up on Schell Isle because he has a job to do. Confused and damaged as he is, silent and withdrawn, Kitten Joe has a function here—what, he does not know, only that it's almost time.

The most troubling thing about it? He can't wait to start.

The arrival of the Little Sisters of the Apocalypse has shaken his psychic machinery into motion. Something about them... Something about them. Memories shift like large shapes in a fog bank.

Lurking in the square during the first encounter, Joe was surprised to hear the sound of his own sadly unused voice, creaking with rust but easy enough to hear; his voice, naming the religious order they represented. He knows them! But from where, and why? *My name was never really Kitten.* Without knowing why, he understands that it is time for him to start preparing the cats for their move into the next phase. At this stage he is not certain how he will accomplish this or how he's supposed to use them. But it is time.

• And in her own welter of conflicting needs and wishes, Charlotte Hagen, acting mayor and erstwhile poet, shakes her head like a tiger stormed by bees. *And in the end the meaning's clear...* my God! It is her next to last line in ROAD KILLS. The hell of it is she cannot for the life of her tell what is going to be the last line of her major poem.

Keep the faith. If you must, dissemble.

Look upon my face and tremble.

Another line has come to her: *And in the end the meaning's clear...* Fine. What comes next? She does not know. She doesn't have a clue.

Perhaps because these are strange times Chag is in an exaggerated state, with every nerve end jangling. Every action seems to mean more than its surface value. People have agendas here.

Chag knows that the head nun, Trinitas, sees beyond the surface Schell Isle presents to her. If she and the others are entrenched in the municipal computer lab, it is for more than the stated reasons. Yes they have a fortification program; they have it in place now and are fine-tuning.

But there's more going on. In times when the sky looks like a spreading bruise and the earth may crack open at any second, when enemies of this world and possibilities not of this world lurk just beyond the horizon, when the decayed civilization drives them out of the cathedrals, the Little Sisters of the Apocalypse are using every means that comes to hand, whether intellectual or spiritual or electronic, to fortify themselves. The lab seems like the right place for this. In the presence of impending chaos, who wouldn't want to set up headquarters in the most sophisticated mainframe available? They recognize one of the best tools devised to enhance human understanding.

Or is it need that draws them?

The nuns are here because they and the women of Schell Isle are all on the verge, Chag thinks.

But what are we on the verge of?

It seems important to her to go and check on the other women.

K.'s mother's right side is paralyzed. She does not speak. Is she still in there? K. wonders: does she know me? The nurses use a chilling

113

technical term that will not comfort. They say she is "aware."

❖

My God, Trini thinks, and then tries hard not to move even though every atom and fibre of her body shivers. She has come out to the edge of the island to pray because she imagined it was the one place she could be alone. "Who's there?"

Naturally there is no answer. Although she holds her breath she is not even certain what it is that she senses, rather than sees. Behind the fringe of scrub palms and stubborn spruces that stands between her and the rest of the island, something or somebody has just left or is just creeping forward. She lets her voice drift over the dried out lakebed. "Who is it?"

Trini is aware that she may be inviting her destiny, but to her surprise she welcomes it. Even if the outcome is bad, at least it will end this odd, strained period of waiting for what she now perceives as violence ready to erupt. Get it out in the open and you can deal with it and have it over with. At least you know what you're here to fight. "Whoever you are," she says to whatever is approaching, "don't be afraid."

❖

Ag is in the local market picking over produce for the sisters when she looks up, catching Nella's furious expression. The rage in the naked glare makes the nun tremble.

"Right. Right," the failed suicide barks, making an imperfect sign of the cross with her right hand. It is clear that she's disturbed—a handsome women so shaken by rage that it

114

makes her voice thick and ugly as she parrots, "The Everlasting has fixed His canon 'gainst self-slaughter."

The stranger's palpable misery makes Ag want to take her by the wrists and beg her to stop doing this to herself but all she can say is, "I beg your pardon?"

Nella picks up a watermelon and smashes it at Ag's feet. "Now get out of my face."

❖

"Fucking bitch," Squiggy says, encased or is it entombed in the safety of his trailer. There is blood on his Stilson wrench. If he didn't jump on Courtney and do the job when he had her alone on the point last week, it was because there was too much going on. Women farting back and forth in a state of excitement because of this aggregation of black leather bitches waiting on the mainland with their silver crosses and their tough motorcycles. It's their fault that he didn't get what he wanted. He could have had his fun with this black-haired government bitch if only he hadn't been interrupted by the arrival.

He hates the nuns for getting in his way like this. He hates them all. Pacing the tiny floor, Squiggy chants in rising frustration. Looping in helpless repetition, the words fall over each other until they grate his throat raw. "Fuck all fucking bitches."

❖

I swim," K. tells her college roommate some months before A.'s terminal diagnosis. "I don't want to have a horrible old age." A. says, "What makes you think you're going to have an old age?"

❖

These are some of the thoughts of Stephanie, who is dying:

—They tell you you're going to die, but they don't say when.

—Or they fall all over each other trying not to mention it.

—I wish it were somebody else.

—I wish it would be over.

—I wish it wouldn't happen at all.

On good days she thinks maybe it isn't happening, but she knows it is. Steph doesn't even have to look into the mirror to see that her color's changed and her body is falling away. There isn't much left now except the skeleton she'll leave behind. She takes fourteen different medications to maintain functions other people take for granted. Look at them lined up next to the checklist, bottles rank on rank on her bedside table. Some are for the disease and others are for the aftereffects of the pills she takes. Because she isn't dead yet Stephanie hopes. She takes her pills. Some days she wakes up feeling good enough to make plans.

Then her body reminds her. She's not going to make it. Please God let me hang in until Larry comes back. She thinks:

—It isn't fair. No. It isn't right that I should want so much to live while all those healthy—God—damned—men—all those healthy fools go happily off to war.

—Men who ruin good bodies on something so —God— damned—*arbitrary*. They've got what I want and they're throwing it away.

—At least it's quick.

Stephanie thinks bitterly, —Given that everybody has to die some day, and given the option, who wouldn't rather go off to war in perfect health and get blown away in one

116

exciting second?

—Maybe Nella ought to get into the war.

Everything she thinks is framed in relationship to men.

When her friend Nella comes Stephanie has to raise herself up in bed and *smile*; she must become a pageant, a celebration of life. Although there are times when Steph wants to beg people to kill her—or keep her alive—she makes a big smile for the sake of her friend. People depend on her for this. It's almost as if the fact she's dying has turned Stephanie into a holy artifact—someone others need to touch or look at to ensure their own good fortune.

—I'm not dying for you. I'm dying for myself.

—I wish they didn't expect so much. I wish they wouldn't say how well I'm taking it. Don't they know I have no choice here?

—I wish they didn't think I was so good about the whole thing. I'd rather be a shitty person and not have to be sick.

Alone, she lets the tears flow through transparent fingers. And then Stephanie, who has indeed been stretched and made into a better person by this ordeal, erases tears and constructs a smile for whoever is.

Here is Charlotte Hagen, radiant with health, Chag with her self-deprecating hello. She grimaces apologetically precisely because she's fine and strong. "I had to come."

It is bizarre. Perhaps because she has somehow become this talisman against misfortune, this sacred object, Stephanie brings out the best in everyone. "I know. I'm glad you came."

Going into the bedroom, going past Stephanie's worried and suffering daughters, Chag has managed to say some mitigating thing to each. "Listen," she says to the grieving girls, "Just let her be herself." She means: *don't force her to be so strong for you*. Yet for all Chag knows it is this show of

117

strength that gives the ugly process of dying some meaning. "Let her get mad if she wants to, let her cry."

Her girls look stricken; it is so hard! "We just want some last words from her."

"Something to take away with us."

❖

Dying, K's friend A. finds her daughters parched for significant last words; because she's still A. she grins instead: "Emily, this isn't a movie."

❖

Chag understands their need to attach some greater meaning to their mother's ordeal—to make it stand for more than its face value. The girls are so young they still think life can be managed, like art. They depend on their mother for memorable last words. They exhaust her, trying to store up last good times.

Chag finds it necessary to demystify Stephanie's death for them. "Just love her and stop trying to make it all make sense."

Chag thinks: *Poor Steph. Dying takes too long.* Either that, or it doesn't take long enough.

❖

Nobody knows what Nella thinks.

There is a dark place in the mind of every suicide that will not yield to anyone. Go there before the fact and return to it again after the fact and it will still be closed to you. Nobody understands what drives a suicide. Nobody. It is enough to say that unhappy Nella notes with a keen, disproportionate sense of irony that death is coming to Stephanie, who has so many people who love her—daughters, the absent husband who idolized her—while Nella, destroyed from the inside out because David left her for another woman, just lives on and on and on.

This is how the men define us. Damn us. Damn them all.

It doesn't matter that David's away at war, he is just as lost to Nella. It's the loss that defines her. Pain and envy. Rage. *If there were no men, I wouldn't be like this.*

"I want you to be all right," Chag tells her firmly, Chag, who knows nothing of what she is feeling. And Nella? She just smiles and nods. People always try to jolly the suicide: you are all right, aren't you? Aren't you?

The truth is stark.

Don't think you are like me. Don't even presume to know me.

❖

A. thinks what's happening to her is part of an organic scheme for the universe, her body governed by nature, to which it will return without a struggle, while K. argues for the affect that human will can exert. Although she will outlive A. by four years, K.'s mother is beyond argument.

❖

Years from now, when both deaths have been accomplished, the daughters of both Nella and Stephanie will dream of loss and rejection—the train pulling out from the platform with their mothers waving goodbye while they who needed them the most are left behind. They'll remember their mothers in

119

their sweet moments and grieve for the close times they should have had together. They will dream that their mother is flying. They will dream that their mother is restored to them in full health and happiness, forever young.

It is they who will have to get old. And stop being pretty as time takes hold of them.

❖

Courtney thinks there's something creepy about a bunch of women who don't even *think* about sex. "Like it or not, tool or weapon, it's there," she shouts at Ag in the marketplace without explanation, and is surprised when the nun turns away with a knowing grin.

Courtney thinks that this Trini, the head nun, has it in for her, and what pisses her off most is that without makeup, even in those grungy clothes, with hair that looks like she's combed it with a fork, this Trini is a beautiful woman. Courtney gets the idea that this Little Sister of Whatever knows her for what she is, which is by no means autonomous. Filled with hate as she is, angry and resentful, Courtney's hooked on men and can't kick the habit, and it pisses her off that this Trinitas *who could care less* can look in her eyes and know.

She thinks that now that Chag has let these weird, other-directed women into the Schell Isle mainframe, there's no getting rid of them. And Courtney knows that she and the nuns are at cross purposes. She doesn't know what they want, exactly, but she knows that sooner or later she and the holy sisters are going to be at loggerheads.

❖

Nobody cares what Squiggy thinks—and Kitten Joe? Nobody knows what goes on in the head of this strange, mute exile, not even Kitten Joe, who paces with his hands pressed together in some long-unused gesture whose purpose he no longer remembers. Going to the tiny bathroom in his shack he looks for clues in his face, leaning into the mirror in an attempt to bring it back, but it's like looking for clues in the face of a bombed-out planet.

❖

"Come here," Courtney says to Squiggy, who has come in to help her move file cabinets from her office at home into the bedroom. "I want to tell you something."

Squiggy knows what that means—the sweet come-on. With all the men gone, it's playtime for good old Squiggy here. He'd rather have had it his way, in the sand with the blood drying on the wrench and her screaming No No at him, but, Hey. This haughty bitch is coming on to him!

You called? With a bump and a grind he fetches up against Court and plants his open mouth on hers with his tongue busy: SMACK. It is like running aground on a coral reef. Her long nails rip the soft part of his neck. Hurt and angered, he yips. "What *is* this?"

"Wait a minute," she says. "Lay back. Not yet."

"What the fuck, what the fucking..." Squiggy is smouldering.

"First you have some things to do." Courtney leans forward to give instructions in a whisper because she has enemies. She knows she has enemies. Even here she cannot be certain whether the room's been bugged since the morning's sweep. She begins in a conversational tone. "All in good time, if that's what it takes, OK? You want me? Fine."

Squiggy breathes harder.

"But first you have to prove that you're a real man. Listen carefully."

Squiggy leans in.

He will not see Courtney's look of disgust as she whispers, "I have a job for you."

"And I'll get…"

"Police protection," she says.

❖

Chag is making her rounds on the island, checking with the various women without being sure why she needs to do so. She intended to visit even Courtney, but at the sight of Squiggy's motor scooter canted against the ornamental mailbox outside her house, she backs off. Not today.

What do we have to say to each other anyway?

She wants to see to her people, she needs to know they are *all right*, but Courtney's doors are locked to her.

Chag comforts herself with a couple of newfound lines. She is not sure where they will fit in the scheme of her uncollected poems but here they are.

Beginning or end, the world still glistens;
Something huge stops cold—and listens.

Yes Chag is embarrassed by cliche and the easy rhyme. At the same time she has the idea that life on the cusp of the millennium lends itself to this kind of thing. Sound bytes. Cliches that stand for communication. With the men gone she and the other women on Schell Isle are spinning out their lives in genre units: interchangeable pieces of boilerplate borrowed from a million movies, the narrative bits of which they have made their lives.

In her time Chag has played Nice to Come Home To and Careerist and Lonely Artist, but in the last few days of signs and omens she has been brought back to bedrock. Now she is One Woman Alone. Sees herself in the door to a deserted house like the pioneer woman looking out over the prairie.

Very well, alone.

Early American. American, ready to weather hard times and protect the homestead until she sees her man riding back from the war with his head bare and his right arm dragging as his horse shambles in to the one place where he knows that no matter how far he roams he is missed, and will be welcomed, and never mind that she's had to grub in the snow for last year's parsnips and slaughter the animals to stay alive and has grappled hand-to-hand, fighting to the death with Comanches, or is it rapacious squatters, and meanwhile, where was he? Where was he anyway?

Off at some war.

Very well, alone.

And when he comes back he won't remark on how well she did or how hard it was for her, he'll bury his head in her neck and ask what they all do, "Did you miss me?"

Or is it this, while she looks over his head at the void he is too self-absorbed to recognize, much less acknowledge: "What's for dinner?"

Isn't that the way it goes?

Alone.

If there was ever a time when she could have made an ally of Courtney, it is long gone. Chag drives past the shuttered house with her shoulders high and her head down, understanding that she has not one but two bad enemies now. Doubtless Courtney is in there right now screwing twisted

123

Squiggy like a house afire. From now on he will do anything Courtney wants him to do.

❖

In the deserted pueblo not many miles away from Schell Isle, the Outlaw family sits around a fire. Queenie is angry and deeply troubled because Prince is in another of his interminable trances. Although Queenie has no way of knowing this, he threw out his arms and snapped into place at the precise moment when the electronic barrier to Schell Isle opened for just long enough to let the Little Sisters of the Apocalypse begin streaming over the lakebed.

She does know that these strange outsiders in nun things and leather have ridden onto the island she intends to waste and pillage.

This alone would not bother her. What can they do to hurt her anyway, unarmed, holy bitches? What bothers Queenie is the terrible business of this boy of hers, the vision that grips him. For three days her baby's stood without moving with his arms spread and his back arched, with that great mouth glaring and his eyes rolled back in his head. Seized by something Queenie can't see, Prince won't respond to her touch; he won't sleep and he doesn't eat. He won't even talk to her. He's had these before. She took them to be fits but now Queenie's not so sure. Prince has this *elevated* look, as if he's hearing music from sublime, unseen orchestra.

She can run whiskey or eggs and bacon or naked babes under his nose and shout in his ear and still not budge him.

"Oh please," she whispers because she doesn't want the others to know how upset he is. "We've got to get moving."

124

She hums, "I'll get you a girlfriend," but he still doesn't snap out of it.

Until or unless he does they are going to starve to death in this cavern, because the Outlaw family does not move out until every member is ready. Prince knows this and yet he's gone off wandering in some territory Queenie can't even imagine and when she pulls on his arm and cries and begs, he won't talk to her.

❖

Intent on her own death, Nella ignores Chag's instructions to take care of herself.

Driving aimlessly, she ends at the menacing shack in the middle of the overgrown territory where Kitten Joe hides. She catches the recluse coming out of his shack with a big sack that squirms like a living animal.

"Listen," she says desperately, "I don't know who you are or what you think you're doing out here with all these damn cats but I need something I think you can give me. I want to make a deal."

He turns toward her but says nothing.

In a way, she's grateful that the slouch hat hides his face. This is embarrassing. Grabbing his arm, she clears her throat. "I need to die."

A long silence follows.

"Aren't you going to say something?"

Trapped, the recluse just stands there, waiting for her to be through with him.

"Do you hear me?" Because he does not shake her off or refuse her or even turn his head at the terrible suggestion, Nella spells out her special request. "Look, I even brought a gun for you."

When Kitten Joe still does not move or speak she goes on in greater detail. "Don't you understand? If that's what you get off on, I want to give you the pleasure of killing me."

He won't speak. Can't?

Finally, unhinged by his silence, Nella rakes off the tattered fedora with one angry hand and for the first time looks directly into the face of the recluse. Kitten Joe does in fact hear and it's clear that he comprehends. Standing in the path with his head bare, Kitten Joe regards Nella with such mild eyes that for a second—for a second only—she's shaken in her resolve.

"Oh shit," she says. Nella is touched. No. Staggered, because Kitten Joe has been listening the while with tears coursing down his face and more tears standing in his eyes.

"I'm sorry," Nella says gently, patting him as if that alone will assuage his grief. "I won't bother you again."

Driving back from the point she passes Squiggy, who is just emerging from Courtney's house. It crosses Nella's mind that she could probably get this walking slime to do the job. After all, doesn't he clean cellars and empty cesspools? For enough money this rodent would do anything. She stops the car and gets out. She raises her hand as if to hail him but as the raunchy handyman turns with a complaisant leer, she drops her arm.

His teeth are covered with green scuzz.

I am desperate, Nella thinks, *but I'm not that desperate*.

The smile slides over her like oil. "What do you want, bitch?"

Abruptly, she turns away. "Nothing."

❖

Disgusting bitch. On-again, off-again. I see how your lip curls when you look at me.

Squiggy understands that Nella does not want him to touch her even though he can't guess at the irony. Of all the people on Schell Isle, he's the only one who can give the failed suicide what she wants. In fact he may even have been rehearsing for this moment, because Squiggy alone is angry and savage enough to push her into the arms of her true lover. Death. Murder is nothing to him. Squiggy, who would happily off her in an instant.

Nella goes back to her car, saying hurriedly, "Nothing!"

Something in Nella's look sends him trotting after her. "What is it, babe? You want me to do you?"

She draws herself up. "I don't want you to do anything."

"But you..."

"I'm sorry." Her eyes fill with tears. "I'm sorry!"

"Bitch!"

In the next second she's gone, leaving Squiggy standing in the road behind her, stewing in his own hatred.

"I'll show you," he says. "I'll show all of you."

Traveling overland by car, truck, on horseback, on foot and finally on his knees, the injured survivor has finally made it to the edge of the lake, leaking blood and yet overcoming all odds to reach home. The lake! He'll throw himself into the water and thus get the strength to go on. It's been a long, hard progress from the war to this spot so close to Schell Isle. The injured survivor used to be somebody you know with his own sweet grin and distinctive voice print, but war has changed him into just another soldier. Until he can make it home and throw himself into his woman's arms again, that's all he is. Loved again, he can look into his sweet love's eyes and see himself reflected. Then he'll remember who he is, OK? Only then can he take off the uniform and turn back into a person.

He is the forerunner. Dragging himself along on his elbows the exhausted soldier inches forward, thinking to plunge his face in the water. But. What! The lakebed is bleached and cracked to the texture of the soldier's own ruined face; in the years since he and the others marched away from here, the damn thing has gone dry.

"Oh no," he whispers, no longer strong enough to speak aloud; his lament is for more than the water. "Where has it all gone?"

Grieving, he rolls over into a little gully, putting his mouth to the sand at the bottom in hopes of finding some moisture. This puts him in a slight declivity—not much, but just enough to put him below the level protected by the electronic barrier.

Inching forward on his belly because he does not have the strength to stand erect, the straggler will slip under the electronic barrier without knowing how narrowly he escapes being extinguished in a blaze of light like a mosquito in a patio bug zapper.

Watch him broach the sandy lakebed, making the long approach to Schell Isle on his knees and elbows because he's too weak to make it to his feet. This man has suffered much and sacrificed everything to get this far; he's gone through fire and flood and narrowly escaped death in ruined cities. He's survived disease and weathered fevers that rose when his wound festered. He's sacrificed everything to get here. He did it for the woman he loves.

The returning soldier pushed himself past the limits of his endurance to get here, fell and got up and fell again and struggled to his knees to keep moving because he promised the woman he loved that he'd come back to her. At least he thinks he did. War has a way of softening the past and distorting memory. Remember your love in its best moments; forget the things she said to you. When all about you are losing theirs you have to believe that you're suffering for something that's worth fighting for. In the sweet haze that time and distance build between separated lovers, everything's idealized; the woman he left behind, his excitement at leaving.

This starving veteran is fueled by the memory of his beloved's face, the scent of her hair. It's the only thing that's kept him going.

Now it's time. Her love will make him strong. His darling will hold him and love him and make him well.

By dawn the returning soldier has almost reached the island, where he expects to be recognized and welcomed and taken in by the woman whose picture he's kept pinned in his heart. Beautiful, softest, lovely. They had such good times. God! He wants her to make him whole again. But an armed woman approaches in the pink early morning, striding out across the lakebed.

Robert, for it is Courtney's lover Robert, rises to his knees. It's her! He sees her! *Courtney, dearest!* The culmination of his dreams. "My darling dear. Thank God it's you!" Sobbing, he holds out imploring arms to his beloved Courtney, who is assessing him with a general's squint. He says weakly, "Honey, I'm home."

Does she recognize him?

Does she hear his loving cry?

It is unclear.
It makes no difference.
A man!
"Fuck!"
She shoots him through the head.

7

When she got it together and girded herself for this expedition, Queenie Outlaw did it with a high heart. She strapped her favorite leather vest around her lusty, spreading body and laced on her boondockers over leather pants; she put on her best studded jacket and chose the red leather helmet with the reflective face plate and the racing flame pattern painted in gold along the sides.

When you go out to get 'em, you want to look *good*.

And she looked magnificent. When she got into the first vehicle and moved them out she felt like one of the early pioneers setting out to find the west. The Outlaws were ready for anything, even the Donner Pass.

Now, shit!

Island public radio tells Queenie that not only are the Little Sisters of the Apocalypse posted on Schell Isle, the women are beefing up fortifications with the help of these computer jocks in nun suits. Queenie does not know what this means, but right before he klunked and fell out, transfixed, her boy Prince whirred, shouting: *Lay back*.

They've laid back for too long. The sheen is off Queenie's helmet and her leather pants are beginning to smell.

She is pacing the biggest room in the undiscovered pueblo

where she and the others have been holed up for what's stretched into days. The Outlaws are the first white people to find this place. Indifferent to her surroundings, focused on her own problems, Queenie crunches over an anthropologist's treasure of axes and arrowheads and potshards, pulverizing history with every step. Ghosts stir; winds whine in the chimney and the painted eyes of the painted wolfshead on the adobe wall begins to glow; in her discontent she may even have aroused the Great Spirit and made him angry, but Queenie doesn't know it.

If she did she wouldn't care. The Pueblo heritage means nothing to her. Same deal. She's lost her own heritage. Those assholes with bulldozers smashed their shacks and ground the past out of existence. So what else is new?

The Outlaw daughters and their men have retired to other rooms to grumble and make love. While their discontented wives play poker for clothes, her other sons are down in the canyon playing laser tag with real weapons; since morning Earl has lost an inch off the top of his Mohawk and Lord's right bicep is singed.

She thinks, bitterly, *At least they're awake*. Which is more than she can say for Prince. Without food or sleep her favorite has been standing there for days. It's as if all his systems have shut down, everything that keeps Prince going focused and turned inward, fueling his intense concentration.

What does he see? What the fuck does he see anyway?

Prince isn't asleep, exactly, but he is in no way aware of his mother's attempts to rouse him. If he did know, would he care? Probably not. He's locked safe inside himself, in a place where neither his mother nor evil spirits can reach him. Therefore even when she pushes, Prince keeps the exact same position with his arms spread and his back arched and his huge pale irises fixed on God knows what. He's been standing here for three days like a totem.

Queenie puts her thumb in a Coke bottle and shakes it and squirts it in his face to keep his mouth from drying up. When he does not flinch at the spray she steps closer and says, "Son?"

But Prince is long gone. She always knew he was strange. What is she doing with this wild visionary? What if he never comes back?

Son of a bitch they can't afford to wait. Sit around in this pueblo much longer and they'll run out of supplies, or end up so short that they run out before they even reach their objective. They'll have to go back to the city and provision this outfit all over from the beginning. It could take weeks. Either that or they'll get back to the nest and her kids will dig in and refuse to leave again. All Queenie's best efforts will come to naught. The girls are already sick of travel. The boys are impatient and if you scratched the warlike surface, you'd probably find them ready to let this one go by. No way.

Let this one go by and attrition and inertia will nail the Outlaws to their past. Queenie hasn't come all this way to turn tail and run home. Hell, Schell Isle is her damn home in spite of what they've done to it, and if her kids were too young to care when they got turned out, well tough. She's going to get hers back. She's going to do it or die in the attempt.

She's got to get this show on the road. Frustrated, Queenie shouts into her boy's ear one more time. "Son?"

Prince neither moves nor blinks. When she climbs up on a box and glares into his eyes his great blind stare gives back nothing.

She gives him a kick, shouting. "Prince. Son! Enough is fucking enough." Queenie does not know what holds him there.

When he comes back to consciousness even Prince won't know.

In the dream visited on him during this strange period Prince finds himself lying in soft, deep grass like a featherbed, in a place where there is no pain and no hunger and no more wanting. There's nobody around. In the dream something is just about to happen; it is going to happen soon! Although Prince is alone in the dream he is completely happy in the expectation. There is an unimaginably beautiful lover somewhere nearby, just out of sight.

When he comes back to himself the sense of loss will be so intense that it makes him want to weep. Bereft, Prince will keep this to himself because Outlaws always stick together, they're strong and tough and they're proud. When they move, they move out all at once. And beyond—unless it's above—this, Outlaws never cry. Still, even though he is going to live to be a very old man who has several wives and many grandchildren, Prince will wonder about this lost vision and pine for it for the rest of his life.

Dying, he is going to smile and hold out his arms to it.

"Fuck this shit," Queenie says. She summons her family with one blast on the ram's horn she has found in a corner of the pueblo. She will not know or care which Indian spirits this raises. Or which it angers. At a signal from her the Outlaw men and their women hoist Prince on their shoulders like an outsized log, a statue of himself. They haul him out and throw him in the back of the lead truck, where he rattles amid canisters of nerve gas. As they form up and go hurtling across the desert on the last leg of this assault mission, Prince's

134

position changes slightly.

If she weren't too driven and angry to notice, Queenie would see this in the rear view mirror: Prince has put his rigid right hand in front of him and raised the blade edge in either admonition or benediction. It's impossible to know.

No matter; riding along in the back of a truck like a felled bronze, Prince has already fulfilled his function by delaying them. If there is a design, he is part of the design. The Outlaws are not the underclass for nothing. Snorting, Queenie would suggest that they are what they are because they won't knuckle under to convention. If this is the case, the conventions have been constructed to make life hard for them.

In the cosmic scheme of things, who decides who gets to call the shots?

When you march to a different drummer it's hard to know when you're making a misstep. As they have from the beginning of time as Queenie and her family measure it, time and events and the society conspire against the Outlaws.

No matter what happens next or how it comes down, their arrival is, as it has been forever in the history of the family, exquisitely mis-timed.

In one of those last-minute judgment calls provided by life and reinforced by the nature of narrative, Queenie and her ugly brood are—again!—a half-beat off.

They will arrive at Schell Isle seconds too late.

❖

Everybody's too preoccupied to watch the phenomenal skies—silver at night and in the mornings, purple. Strange silhouettes whiz past. Signs. Wonders. Everything is changing.

❖

Behind Chag's back and against her orders, Courtney is raising an army. Fueled by Courtney's suspicions and accelerated by the arrival of the nuns, the idea catches fire. Although some of the women refuse to admit exactly who they are arming against, they turn up at the police station to get instructions and to check out the weapons Courtney has stacked in the administrative offices.

She begins to lead forays out to the deserted point for target practice and it is no accident that one of the targets is the tin smokestack on Kitten Joe's shack. If the cats are disturbed the women have no way of knowing. When a bullet pings off the smoke stack nothing happens. No cats come running out. Even when somebody aims too low and accidentally nicks the rooftree, Kitten Joe doesn't show himself.

Some of Courtney's armed women have tied red scarves around their arms just above the elbows. Others wear identical red hats identically tilted over the eye at a belligerent angle. In the absence of an official uniform, the women make these tokens stand for the uniform, but they take them off when they come back into town because Courtney's tactics dictate secrecy.

Some things need to grow in the dark.

Still there are women who suspect what their friends are up to. They shake their heads unhappily. Something's going on that they don't know about and they don't like it. Nothing they can put their fingers on exactly, but they know that something's up.

Political discussion abounds—women feeling each other out. The women who side with Courtney say to their friends:

"You want him back? You want him back to take over your job and mess up your life?"

Backing off from the extreme, Chag's people answer: "This isn't the enemy you're talking about. These are our *men*." The moderates look at their sisters in a complex pride: *You* may have problems with your man, but I know how to handle him.

"Try monsters/slavedrivers/rapists/domineering assholes..." the list goes on and on.

To a woman the moderates ask: "What's he ever done to you, that makes you so murderous?"

The answer isn't always forthright. It throws the questioners back on themselves, so that after these debates each side is left brooding. This is the question the militants put into the air:

"What hasn't he done?"

Anger feeds on anger and training in secret, the army grows.

❖

Brought back from death, K.'s friend M. is making herself strong. Welcome back, M.'s friends say, but M. makes no promises and no plans beyond Thursday.

❖

"What?" Chag wakes in the night, trembling. "Who's there?" When she turns on the lights she finds the bedroom is empty; so is the rest of the house. When she goes to her window she sees nothing on her property has changed but there is something going on next door, the. The. The ground is moving. No. Something is. Animals! The ground is thick with the seething backs of small animals. When her eyes adjust so she can make out what's happening, Chag starts laughing out of sheer excitement and nervousness. It's either funny or it is not funny.

In its own way it is marvelous.

As Chag watches, Kitten Joe turns to face her lighted window and then, unperturbed by the knowledge that she sees everything, the recluse shrugs and goes back to his business. He puts down the heavy sack he must have lugged all the way across the island and he unties the rope that kept it shut. Quick as water running downhill, cats slither out, their sleek backs shimmering in the moonlight. How many other loads of cats has he brought?

Cats are everywhere. The entire area around Courtney's house is carpeted with cats: velvety, pervasive.

In the next second the lieutenant's lights go on and the alarm system kicks in. If the Little Sisters have beefed up the island's security systems, they may have tampered with the alarm link to Courtney's property. Or not. Either way, her private system sounds the alert, but too late.

Instinct makes Chag turn out her own light because she does not want Courtney to catch her watching. There would be questions. If somebody has broached Courtney's system, shouldn't Chag report it? Why hasn't she? Indeed, why doesn't she pick up the phone now, or tap a message into her computer terminal?

Partly, it's the wish to see what will happen next. But more important is this. Strange as he is, remote and driven—even though they don't know each other and have never ex-changed words—Chag likes Kitten Joe better than her stormy lieutenant.

As lights sweep Courtney's house and warning whistles shriek, Joe's cats race for a hole in the foundation. Quicker than bath water going down the drain they disappear into it. By the time Courtney comes to her balcony to find out what's going on Kitten Joe is gone. The cats have vanished. The yard is empty and there's no indication that it was ever anything but empty.

When the police cars come Courtney looks briefly in Chag's direction even though she can't see her adversary standing in the window of her darkened bedroom. While Courtney paces, her military police sweep the house and come up empty. If Chag is watching and listening she'll see Courtney's agitation as she presses them: *are you sure?* and the women's impatience: *Certain. Nobody there. No sign of anybody. Nothing.* Shaking her head, Courtney sends her people back to headquarters.

❖

In the morning everything marches in the usual way, people going to their offices, Chag off to work in the municipal building, Courtney to police headquarters to welcome new recruits. The armed women Courtney has drilled to guard the perimeter of the island are trotting off to relieve last night's shift, and on their motorcycles, various of the Little Sisters of the Apocalypse ply back and forth without any apparent knowledge of the conflicted feelings they inspire in so many of the people here.

A number of women on the island dislike the nuns in spite of the fact that they are doing necessary work. The sisters are nice, at least everybody who talks to them says they are; they're clean, they're quiet. They keep out of people's way

139

and the women who do talk to the sisters report that they haven't once mentioned going to church or even dropped hints about religion. But still.

Many of the women find them creepy.

This is what their enemies say:

—The nuns don't *do* like other people; they aren't interested in the same things.

—History associates them with the arrival of bad times.

—In the plague years, wasn't it the nuns who used to wash the dead? So, what. Are they like, here like vultures?

—Is it true that they can steal your spirit through the keyhole while you sleep?

—If these nuns don't clear out, and soon, something heavy is going to happen here.

The Little Sisters are aware of the animus and don't try to fight it. They proceed serenely; after all they have work to do. The only sign they give is a slight intensification of concentration, an acceleration of effort—that and the fact that although their enemies don't know it and probably wouldn't like it, at night the Little Sisters pray for them. Threaten the nuns, tell them not to pray for you *or else*, hit them and they'll pray for you anyway.

❖

No one, no doctor, no nurse, no attendant at any point in seven years says outright what's going on with K.'s mother. They treat death symptomatically.

❖

Celibates though they are, the nuns signify the return of the

140

men. Courtney's sure of it. Celibacy: another of those things men define by their presence. Without them it would be a non-event.

No wonder Courtney hates them.

Even so she is grateful to the Little Sisters for early warnings: The current order is about to change. Forewarned, she's raised a considerable army to fight the Return. She numbers the angry and the bitter women among her followers, along with many of the stolid Status Quo people who like the extra room in the bed, the uncontested household.

What consolidated Courtney's resolve? The fact that when she saw her lover Robert raising his arms to her in adoration she took him as the first drop of rain that signals the deluge and she didn't like it. Her last doubts disappeared. Even when his eyes brightened at the sight of her and he held out loving arms, even as her mouth dried out and her loins caught fire Courtney knew she would never take her lover back. *Sex!*

Sex. Enraged by the sight of him she thought: *Who needs it?*

The trouble was, her body wanted it.

Robert, who waited on his knees with his heart in his eyes. Robert, who made her body remember in spite of all her resolve. Need swept her like a disease, acute and prurient.

Courtney, who's spent all these years making herself strong.

No wonder she nailed him on the spot.

I don't need you. For the moment, she believes it. *Now I'll never need anyone.*

She's free. With Robert dead, Courtney is completely independent. Full of her own powers. Never again will she let herself be defined by a man. No. Diminished. Look, she hates the thing that leapt in her loins and made her go all weak when she saw him, the need that flickers there now in spite of her furious efforts at denial. You bet she had to blow him away. She'd do it again in a minute.

Listen. If she needs sex, there's always Squiggy—just as soon as he's done this little job for her. His payback for helping her get rid of the nuns. It was Courtney's idea, but Squiggy's imagination caught fire. He has clear thoughts about where to begin. By the time he finishes the job and word gets back, these holy babes in black will be so freaked and disgusted that they'll pack up their laptops and roll out without wasting time with goodbye and thank you.

I'll celibate you, she thinks bitterly.

Without needing to spell it out, Courtney knows if she can just get rid of the nuns she can forestall the Return. Push leads to shove and she thinks they're here to make it happen. If these willful virgins are the men's ticket home, she's going to tear up the ticket. With them gone all the men in the world can wail at the barrier and it won't make any difference. Put something precious in place and walk away from it and you'll be damn sure it won't be there when you get back. Or it won't be yours any more.

Now the island is ours.

Her and Squiggy's plan serves a dual purpose: getting rid of the nuns and bringing down that holier-than-thou head nun Sister Trinitas with her high-handed autonomy. Courtney hates Trini; she hates the intelligence and the sexual independence and she hates her for her visionary glare.

The sisters' improvements on the island's operating system

have been complete for several days. Everything they've done since has been fine tuning. Now even that is complete. In spite of Trini's orders to let it play as long as possible, they've run out of reasons to stay. Perpy would like to get back to the convent mainframe because she wants to load new programs she's gotten from the Schell Islanders; she has several new questions she wants to put to it. Lucy has an idea for a program that would prevent domestic violence: just punch in your feelings here, instead of punching out your wife. She knows there isn't going to be much domestic violence until or unless the men come back but she'd like to get started on it, in case. Ag's just plain sick of being someplace where it's clear they aren't wanted. Trini doesn't mind the way the Acting Governor scowls at her, but Ag minds.

Several others of the sisters have reported incidents: certain things shouted as they rode by on their motorcycles, graffiti, the dead chicken Ag found lashed to her handlebars, rotten apples thrown at them, tacks hammered into their tires.

Now Trini's lieutenants confront her while the other sisters cluster in an anteroom to wait, making it clear that they endorse what's going on.

Because they have been friends for the longest, blunt Sister Agatha puts it to Trini, "It looks to me as if we've done about all we can here."

Lucy adds, "I think the welcome mat's been rolled up."

Trini looks from one to the other. This is a concerted effort then. Trini wonders: have they rehearsed? Probably. Everything is beautifully timed.

Perpy says, "I don't like the looks I get from some of these people." At Trini's puzzled expression she barks, "We offend them, OK? Are you surprised at that? Are you really surprised?"

Agatha is probably thinking of Nella, who acts as if she's scared the sisters will get hold of her soul and force her to go on living. Ag says, "I think they're afraid we are going to start messing in their lives."

Trini shrugs.

Lucy says, "The storekeepers have cut off our Mastercharge. The gifts have stopped. We're asking for trouble if we stay."

Perpy says, "All we want is to go home, where we can pray."

"You can pray here."

Ag says with force, "Home where we can pray in peace, OK?"

Trini cuts her off. "We won't be here much longer."

"Does that mean we can pack it in?"

"Not yet."

Agatha is grim. "We've outlived our usefulness and we've overstayed our welcome..."

"But we're not finished here."

"...And you know it."

Troubled, Trini repeats, "We're not finished here." Pressed to identify and explain what piece of unfinished business keeps her here, would she know what to say? She doesn't think so. She only knows it is the case. In the scheme of divine schemes, she has to say nothing, and hope they'll stick with her.

Lucy grumbles, "If this is a spiritual exercise, I think it's already served its purpose."

"Offer it up," Trini says.

"Dammit, Trini..."

Trini raises her hand: wait. "There's one more thing we

have to do. Just one."

Ag snaps. "Like what?"

"I don't know exactly, I…"

"Come *on*!"

"Something for these people. It's." Trini crosses her hands in the time out signal. How can she explain when she doesn't know?

Perpy brightens. "We could go back home and pray for them."

"That isn't it."

"We could pray for consensus," Ag suggests.

"This isn't a consensus situation." Trini loves them but she can't stay in this room with her friends and colleagues another minute. Not now. She has to get out of here. She needs to be alone. Even more, she needs to pray. She is hard put to explain herself to the other sisters; she isn't even sure what's going on, but she cannot shake the idea that there is something more for her to do here on Schell Isle, some design she is expected to fulfil.

Riding in to this place, Trini thought it would hit her in the eye: what is expected, but they've been here for days now and she still doesn't know. If it won't come to her, she thinks regretfully, she's going to have to go out looking for it.

❖

Her mother is still alive but unreachable. It's clear there's nothing more she can do. K. tiles the kitchen floor. Mows the yard. Starts another novel. Narrative is power.

❖

Plying back and forth across the island in search of whatever comes next, Trini may suspect she's being watched.

❖

By this time Courtney's army is made up of perhaps half the population of the island, including women you wouldn't expect. She has raised her army by fanning panic. She tells the women that the men are going to swarm down on them like the wolf upon the fold and they're in danger.

"Arm yourselves or die."

The women will all nod piously and say yes yes, but they know this is not the real reason.

Courtney's blown hers out of the water but few among the others can shake their man.

He's hard to take sometimes, but he loves her. Is hers to abuse and dispose of, use and misuse and love and keep or throw away; she has to decide!

He'll come running toward her with his arms out, trampling the dried-out lakebed with his heart high and his arms spread wide; he'll be bearing presents, a plundered necklace or an ear taken from a dead civilian, a bit of ribbon from the enemy's uniform. He'll come stumbling through the flowerbeds and knocking over ornaments with his rifle as he turns without remembering that he's still armed, scattering shards of china and tracking mud on the living room rug. He may be wounded, ailing, worse; he may be weak from loss of blood, but he will be laughing and running joyfully, and still the women arm themselves.

To a woman she can hear him. *Baby, don't you know I love you?*

They arm themselves all the same.

146

Ask her if she wants him back and she'll say, —Not until I'm good and ready, but that isn't what she means.

She will never forgive him for leaving.

Here are some of the reasons the women give for resisting the return of the men:

—I can't stand losing him twice.

—Not now, when I've just gotten used to this.

—It's simpler/quieter/nicer without him.

—I'm too used to having the house to myself.

—The whole place is neater. Life is neater.

—I like being on my own.

—It's so peaceful.

—He used to get really mad.

—He was bigger so he always won.

—Life is an even contest now.

Here are some of the real reasons.

—Yelling and snoring.

—Being scared at night.

—His ego; he took up so much psychic *space*!

—With him gone, nobody makes me cry.

They are valid reasons all. And the reasons they want the men back?

Even the women who most want their men back would tell you all of the above is absolutely true. In spite of which, they are anxious for the Return. The pros are less clearly articulated than the cons. They are fuzzier, as they come from the heart.

—I miss him. I miss him a lot.

—I miss him *so much*.

Acknowledging all the above reasons why they do *not* need this, the women who want him back go on to say:

— I just do.

147

Some will add,
—I can't help it. I just do.

❖

Courtney's army is made up of the angry and serene, the rejected and the lovelorn and the satisfied, the damaged and the whole. Her army are prepared to fight the returning men with guns and explosives, with an armory of mace and firebombs cached in basements and sidearms stashed in kitchen cabinets. Wearing the uniforms only in private, the militants will not reveal themselves until the circumstances call for it. Until then, they wait.

In the absence of a better general Courtney calls the shots. At the signal from Courtney, they will ride out.

What about the women Courtney approached who fobbed her off by saying they had to think it over, the indeterminate number who are undecided and the smaller number who may indeed be counted on to help the men? What about the women who refused her outright, and what about the women Courtney knew better than to ask? Here is the sum of their reasons for wanting the men to come back.

—I want him. Don't ask why, I just do.

❖

Vicarious atonement. Trini shudders. Is there something going on here that she doesn't know about? Aware only that what will happen—*will happen*, she prays there is not.

❖

What does Chag want? It is complex. She knows Courtney is fortifying the island even as the nuns perfect the security system. She probably knows about the army but she pretends she doesn't. This is a tactical decision. She knows it won't really exist until or unless she provokes a confrontation.

She may know that Courtney's personal arms race has something to do with the Return, but she has no way of knowing that the Return is coming soon. There have been no messages from the front. Aside from the stir in the air, the unshakable sense of *imminence*, there have been no signs. Nothing a person can point to.

The one piece of concrete evidence has been destroyed. After she shot Robert, Courtney dragged the body into a gully and buried it with a detonator attached to enough explosives to blow up the entire Point. Nobody saw.

For Chag at the moment, the Return is not the issue. The safety of the Little Sisters is the issue here. She's heard things, women grumbling in the center of town. There is the cache or is it treasure trove of moiling cats stashed under Courtney's house. There is the accelerating mystery of Kitten Joe.

Does he mean the sisters harm?

Somebody does.

Chag's not sure how she knows this, but she knows. She knew it even before Court dragged in her fetishes, before certain unpleasant things started happening. There have been signs. Anonymous threats. Crosses crudely scratched into the dirt and then smeared with dog shit. Tracks in the sand under the window to the computer lab.

For their own good, Chag thinks. No, for their own safety, she's going to have to ask the Little Sisters of the Apocalypse to quit the island.

As for the Return: nobody's said anything directly, but the

air is filled with it. Women speculating. It's been so long! Chag can't help but wonder herself. Will it be wonderful or terrible? She misses Toby so much she can't bear it, but the self-protective part of Chag thinks it is too soon.

It's just too soon for the Return. Things are too torn up now, everybody's distracted. Nobody's ready. And there is the secret fear she hesitates to name:

If the men come back and Toby isn't with them, Chag will die of it. And if he is with them? She may still die.

I can't stand to lose him twice.

It's true, she can't. The first time almost destroyed her. She's only lately gotten herself put back together. Look here. With Toby gone she's gotten a lot of work done. Here's Chag with her unwritten poems bubbling near the surface, ready to be realized. With Toby gone she's thrown all her energies, her hopes and desires, everything she has into an orgy of creation that has left her near completion, everything written except the climactic last line of her last poem.

Remember, where this central piece of material is concerned, Chag is close but close only.

Pulling into her parking spot at the municipal building, she mulls it:

And in the end the meaning's clear.

What's the rest? What is it?

She is tired of running along after something that is forever running along ahead, just out of sight and forever out of reach.

Maybe I should have been a nun, she thinks, but she knows that isn't it. Chag does not yet know what she should have been.

But she has arrived at her office. She plunges in the door just as Trini plunges out, looking distracted and driven.

"Stop," Chag says, trying to warn her. Hasn't this Little Sister of the Apocalypse seen the warning signs? It will not occur to her that sometimes a woman has to see the warnings and proceed anyway, rushing to her destiny in spite or because of them. Things are coming to a head here. Chag reaches for Trini's arm. "Wait. There's going to be trouble."

Trini barges past as if her heart is set on it. Driven, rushed and urgent, careless of everything except her need to complete the scheme she cries, "I know!"

❖

"Faster," Queenie shouts to the others, communicating by radio. Each vehicle is driven by somebody she loves—another Outlaw expelled from the land of promise, forcibly ejected from the grand scheme of prosperity, each of them springing into action now after years spent eddying in a backwater outside the mainstream of life.

"Faster," Queenie trumpets, trying to close the distance between them and their target, or destination, but with every mile the Outlaws travel toward Schell Isle they seem to have farther and farther to go.

In a dazzling second of self-knowledge Queenie sees her tragedy in its entirety: she is too ugly for ordinary men but that has more to do with the way she is than the way she looks.

In the kingdom of the blind...

No. This is not her real problem. Queenie's real problem is that she has spent her life in a posture of rebellion, won't wear clothes ordinary people wear, won't say what they say or do like they do, won't do this, refuses to line up for that. Set her down facing one way, according to your expectations, and Queenie's automatic switch sends her careering in the opposite direction. Her kids have been brought up this way so they don't answer to anybody now, not even Queenie. Fighting the established order, Queenie Outlaw has arranged her life and schooled her children in brutal hostility so completely that—son of a bitch!

When the big moments come, she and hers are chronically seconds too late.

In its earliest manifestations, the Outlaws were always next in line behind the person who got the job. It could have been chance; it could have been habit; maybe it was fate. They never heard the news, won the race, got where they were going in time to get the free samples or the large cash prize.

In the matter of the final charge, or is it last stand, the Outlaws' natural recalcitrance is coupled with the delay caused by Prince's mysterious coma. The vision or the seizure that pulled him up out of his seat and hung him on air in the middle of the pueblo. Supernatural? Queenie can't know.

All she knows is that they're about to be late for the biggest event in their lives.

"Laaaaaate," she screams with her head out the truck window. The words trail behind her like a banner in tatters, tearing until they lose themselves in the wind. "Faaaaaster," she bellows, and this follows all her urgings into the void. No matter; nothing can make her entourage roar and rattle along any faster than it is. Still Queenie shouts, desperate because fate is gaining on her. "Late!"

The problem has reached cosmic proportions.

Queenie's about to arrive too late for the rest of her life. Like a train pulling out of a station, life is going to gather steam as they approach—and roar away, leaving her stranded on the platform. Shit!

"Faster," Queenie cries, and in her distress is only faintly aware that the Outlaw vehicles are overtaking a straggling fleet of crippled or disabled cars. Trucks painted in camouflage colors are crawling along as the Outlaws roar past. They rattle along past dusty tanks and trucks and miserable, grimy stragglers on foot, hardly noting that some mass troop movement is headed for the island in such disarray that there's no telling whether it represents a single group or a dozen groups. "Faster," Queenie shouts in blind excitement. Army trucks get in their way; they're about to be mired in the stream of limping cars. "Get out of the way you damn fools. We're almost there!"

...Too late?

Poor Queenie; she has girded herself and put on her best helmet and mobilized her family for a grand encounter, and now—. Without even being aware of it Queenie has run up on the wheels of the last remnants of the long-lost legion of men. Absorbed in their own obsessive search for vengeance against the beautiful, successful women of Schell Isle, Queenie and hers are sucked in and swept along with the limping wagons and broken down Jeeps and tanks of the returning army of defeated and diminished men.

Instead of arriving in time to forestall or prevent it, Queenie is caught up in the Return.

❖

K.'s mother spent her life waiting for a man who never came back in this life. Better believe she is going to meet him, just not here.

❖

153

Queenie thinks fast: can she make this army serve as her Trojan horse? The vehicle of her revenge? She does not know. Confused and frustrated, she screams at the staggering army: "Get out of my way, you damn fools. Out of my way!"

She can hear the voices of her children and their mates in her earphones:

"Hey, Ma."

"Queenie."

"Hey?"

By this time Prince is revived; he is frothing and thrashing in the back of the truck. Hammering on the glass that separates driver and passenger with his mouth stretched wide: *Mother*. He's trying to tell her something that he knows; he's trying to tell her something important, but Queenie's too excited and driven to notice and if she did, there's no time to stop and consult with her visionary son. Late for all the big encounters of her life, she is in a frenzy to outrun her destiny. She will do anything to make up for it. Seeking help from the god of wrath or vengeance, she prays, if Queenie ever prays: *Oh please God, don't let us be late again.*

But her grown kids's voices are humming in her headphones as they ask, "What shall we do?"

She does not know. She does. Queenie leans into her phone and rallies them with a gallant, brassy shout. *"Run on!"*

8

In spite of due warnings, Trini is on her way to the last isolated spot on the island. She knows she is in danger but she has to go. What is at work here?

Fate?

Narrative inevitability?

The hand of God?

Whatever the motivating force, whatever Trini's real or imagined reasons for coming to Schell Isle and for staying when the world tells her to go, it is about to work itself out.

Fixed on solitude, bent on it, she's left the main road and veered off the dirt road, tearing along the sandy path to the place where she goes to meditate. In spite of the terrain she is going almost 70 when her bike hits the tripwire and she spins out, separating from her Harley in midair and landing in the bushes with a terrifying *splat*.

Hurtling through the air she thinks: *Oh God, not this*, just before she hits the ground, thinks it when she has been taught to pray: *Not my will but thine*. She regains consciousness just as her assailant reaches her. "You!"

"Somebody has to do it," Squiggy says.

Sacrifice. It blinds her. *We were called here for a sacrifice*.

Death would be noble and fine. Death would be welcome.

This is not what Squiggy has in mind.

Trini hardly feels the damage her body's sustained so far. The agony comes from knowing what's coming. She prays that Squiggy will beat her to death first. After she gets out of this damn body she won't care what he does to it.

Squiggy raises fists like crossed mallets. He'll grind into her, he thinks, but not before he makes her bleed and cry. Then he'll make her beg. He wants her awake. When he gets down to it, he wants the bitch to know it and know it good.

Trini screams "No!" as Squiggy closes in, hammering on her with both fists, slapping her one way and then that because sex is sex but he can wait. Sex is sex, Squiggy thinks, punching, slapping, but this... Violence carries him farther than he planned.

God, no, Trini thinks, outraged, and then, bloody and rattled hard by Squiggy's unremitting jackhammer blows but still conscious, she is abruptly, unexpectedly...
...

...removed from her body and set free so that she sees beyond and through the present. She is like an escaped soul hovering near the ceiling of an operating room while frantic doctors labor over the shell below.

What Trini sees:

She sees infinity. She sees it as a brilliant series of concentric whorls in which the souls of the multitudes revolve, swirling up and up to the blaze that marks the center, and somewhere near the center she sees her friends; the Little Sisters of the Apocalypse are standing or floating on golden beams rising into or up to the glorious light, and although she only recognizes a couple of their faces, Trini understands that in the end many of the glorified will turn out to be women she knows. Although blood streams from her eyes

156

and she can hardly make them out, Trini sees Agatha and Lucy and Perpetua; she sees the dying Stephanie there and the death-hungry Nella too, both quite near to what she takes to be heaven, and they are beloved; she sees the one is beloved because she has lost everything, and the other because she has thrown everything away; she sees... "Lord Jesus God" Trini cries, elated because she is so close. So *close*. In another minute Squiggy will kill her and she can join the mystic circle. "Some day our friends will be exalted!"

In time, in time.

"Let her go you ugly bastard."

Life intervenes. Trini thuds back into the here and now. Here is vile Squiggy undoing his belt, vicious Squiggy through with his beating and about to begin and as she raises a torn fist to resist Squiggy is gone, his ugly shape replaced by sunlight, Squiggy removed so fast that it is like magic, Squiggy seized by some huge hand and thrown aside. Trini thinks she can hear Squiggy rasping on the ground at some distance, Squiggy broken almost in two, face down and groaning in the dirt and she is glad.

There is a new face hovering above her, new hands trying to raise her carefully so as not to hurt her, light hands wiping the blood from her face, who? She recognizes the shaggy hair and wild beard of the recluse: Kitten Joe. Trini looks again.

She gapes. For the first time the mysterious figure has come close enough for her to see. It is the face the abbot showed her painted on the wall of the cloister, the failed monk or is it desperate contemplative with his existential pain clear even in the picture, and the burned-out eyes. Although she can barely speak Trini croaks: "Brother Jerome!"

At the sound of his name the exiled monk gasps, thunderstruck. "Am I?" And, like Trini, is returned to real life.

The pale eyes are wide and empty as pools. Now in a SNAP—the irises contracting to trap the ultimate picture—the lost monk hurtles back into his own consciousness with a little gasp, soul meeting body like a high diver making a perfect plunge into the pool. To his own astonishment he cries, "My God, you're right."

Trini and the lost monk are returned to life here after being felled by the same vision, brought to earth in the same spot, disparate elements in a scheme that plays itself out but will not reveal itself. But part of a scheme; Trini sees that now. She can't know the nature of the design but she understands she is playing out a larger design.

He shakes his head in wonder. "So that's who I am." Brother Jerome, back from the desert. He looks so sad.

"It really is you."

Bemused, the monk lifts his face to the sky shouting, "Lord, what do you want me to do?"

But Trini is three jumps ahead. She thinks: *If Jerome is here, it's for a reason. We both have business here.* And looking into that brilliant, tortured face she says a prayer for him because without the hat she sees him plain. He looks like one of the early contemplatives, a saint with sockets charred from looking for the face of God, staring too hard into the sun. He got too close!

Although Jerome will not remember anything that led up to or away from the moment of supreme contemplation, or eternal confrontation that almost wrecked him, he knows it is burned into the space behind his retinas, and now that he has returned to his senses he will spend the rest of his life trying to call back the memory of that incandescent second.

Meanwhile they are here. Shaken, the two visionaries, or mystics recognize the eschatological function of events that nobody can understand.

Staggered by the return of memory, Jerome, not Trini, is the injured one here. Although every ligament feels torn and at least three ribs are broken, Trini struggles to sit. Graciously, she extends an arm like a queen bestowing a favor on a courtier, and lets Kitten Joe help her up. "Come," she says gently, because he is astonished, rendered helpless by discovery. "We're needed."

❖

In narrative, if not in life, people can and do end up in the right place when it's time.

❖

By this time everybody knows there is an approaching army on the mainland; vehicles and foot soldiers draw up at the end of the causeway. There is nothing to prevent them approaching over the lakebed once they convince the women to disarm the electronic barrier, but the men stop at the tollgate *pro forma* because they built it and they expect the women to throw the gate wide so they can come in by the causeway.

They expect the women to welcome them with open arms. What man who bravely went to war and staunchly came back to the girl he left behind wouldn't expect her to be grateful?

We're back.

Honey, I'm home.

Aren't you glad to see me?

The silence is profound.

At the toll gate some of the men shuffle restlessly, while others withdraw to consult. They are dusty and bloodstained and broken in places, weary and anxious to get home so they can take off their boots. Right now their hearts are filled with home.

✦

And on the island several things are happening at once.

• Courtney, who has been watching the proceedings on her video monitor at home, sees that the moment is now and heads for her front door, prepared to summon her army. She wants to unleash them and stop this incursion before the group of veterans on the mainland reaches critical mass. She wants to attack before the men figure out that they have enemies here.

• At the toll gate Myrna the guard looks at the men in the front ranks. Their faces are filthy. So are their clothes. If she lets them get close enough she's going to find out for certain that they smell. If they come back now, think how much medical help they're going to need, how many women will be kept awake at night by the men's nightmares, their crying in the night, their need to be told not to be ashamed of what they did, or what they failed to do. Think about muddy boots on the rugs, making room in the bed, think about all that heavy laundry, all those repairs!

Automatically reticent, Myrna tells the men to wait. Then she sits down and taps out the query on her video terminal. She takes her sweet time.

• In her office Chag paces and whirls. They're here. Is Toby with them? Is he not with them? Troubled, she taps out: STALL. She can't or won't make voice contact yet.

None of the women knows what's making them so

160

cautious.

• In the circular tower at the top of her house Verena wheels with her telescope, searching all the distant faces. She finds a face she knows. DADDY? No. It's only Matt. If he comes home now he'll divorce her and move in with Melanie. With a sigh she covers the telescope and turns her back on it.

• A couple of the women try to decide how they will explain the scars Squiggy left on them like a dog scent-marking his territory, bite scars like worms crawling across their soft places.

• Nella rummages in the cellar for her rifle. She hates him. No. She hates herself for still loving him. David. If she sees the bastard she's going to blow him away. If she doesn't see him, she'll blow herself away. Sooner or later she'll blow herself away all the same and that will show them. That will show everyone.

• When her husband left Stephanie looked fine. Terrible things have happened to her since then. Terrible things. Because she's dying to see Larry, and does not want him to see she's dying, Stephanie rakes her fingers down her wasted face and weeps.

Everywhere on the island cabinets are blown open and old memories come tumbling out; it is too much! Everywhere women tighten their mouths and squint.

With him back, everything is going to change.

❖

Helped by Kitten Joe, who has retrieved her Harley and brought her here, Trini makes it to the municipal computer lab and marshals the Little Sisters. "Get your bikes. It's time."

❖

And here is Courtney, who expected to be spearheading the troops at the toll gate at this time. By this time she should be fully armed and on the front lines flanked and supported by her army. Instead she is effectively neutralized. Here is Courtney Ravenal, stern general of a strong and vengeful army, stalled in her front hall, so paralyzed by what she perceives as instruments of evil that she can't even make it to the door. She will be trapped here for the crucial few minutes it takes Trini and the Little Sisters of the Apocalypse to mount their bikes and get to the scene before she does.

Courtney's been held up. She's stalled here even though she's struggling to the door. Time and time again, she tries and is driven back. Now she has on leather pants and riding boots; armed herself with kitchen knives she's trying again, slashing furiously at the living carpet moiling at her feet, twining itself around her ankles, mounting her furniture and baring its fangs and growling at her from the doorframes, the top of the hall mirror, the ledge above the door.

Cats!

Courtney is prevented from launching the crucial assault by the legacy of Kitten Joe.

The cats will not be moved. When nothing else works she takes the lock off her Thompson gun, prepared to spray a path through the animals and walk over their dead bodies.

But as if by prearranged signal, the clot of cats dissolves. Like quicksilver they fragment and melt away, fluid and discrete. Like quicksilver they will meet and flow together again at the end of the inevitable progress to their next assignment—whether here or on some other island is not clear.

Livid, Courtney strides forth. She summons her army from her car phone. All over the island, women are tying scarves above their elbows, arming themselves. They'll all be out by the time she reaches the point where the causeway meets the twin adobe markers that define the gate to Schell Isle. For the moment the women will keep their weapons hidden. At her signal, they'll attack.

❖

Honey?

The men are uncertain now. They've been fighting in enemy territory for months, perhaps years. Grim and terrible as it was, it was fun! There was the sense of power and exclusion, male bonding in the one place she can't go. There they were out in the wild blue, engaged in life-and-death matters every minute and at every level. In time however, a man gets tired of the world without a woman's touch. Now it's time to come home for a little R&R. But the men already intuit that although she wrote them loving letters and sometimes sent them socks and homemade cookies, things are not the same here at Schell Isle.

- Does she still love me?
- Has she forgotten?
- Has she gotten old while I was gone?
- What if she's gotten fat?

After all, it's been a while. She has put her clothes in his closet and moved his fishing trophies out of the living room. She's probably thrown out his stuffed wolverine and the Pontiac hood ornament that he's cherished ever since high school, along with the pictures of certain old girlfriends he used to torture her with.

Thus the men, idly tossing pebbles at the electronic

barrier.

No good at electronics. Simple little—for Pete's sake! What's the matter, has she forgotten how to make the damn thing work? They can't be sure. Is it armed or not?

Hey, is there something the matter here? Where are the open arms and the welcome home dinner I expected here? Hasn't she made me a cake?

Puzzled, the men resort to the old formula. *Are you mad at me?*

The response is as cold as it is immediate. *I'm not mad. Then what's the matter?*

Everything that's fallen between the departure and now quivers in the air between the men and the women they left here for safe keeping: crying in the night, the losses, the sense of betrayal. But she won't tell him this; if he can't figure it out for himself, fuck him. *Nothing's the matter. Everything is fine.*

The barrier crackles.

The gate stays shut.

The front ranks of men eddy, confused. They are weary of war, shattered by the hardship, too spent to be angry any more. They are too proud to beg.

"Son of a bitch," a ragged, outraged woman's voice comes zinging into earphones and out of truck radios, electrifying them. "Aren't you motherfuckers going to do anything?"

Say what? This is a thick, tough, almost androgynous voice. Not one of theirs. Whose is it then? Whose?

The newcomer's voice is frenetic, clotted with rage. "Why don't you bastards get moving? It's time to stop sitting on your thumbs!"

But the men are sick of doing what armies do. All year long they have laid waste and pillaged to keep our country safe for democracy. They've worn out their last pairs of boots and eaten their way through all their supplies. It's time for some R&R.

The voice persists. "If you weak shits won't do anything, I'll have to do it for you!"

Then Queenie, for it could never be anybody but Queenie, bursts through the ranks in her battered truck with the canisters of nerve gas which she has forgotten rolling back and forth in the back along with Prince, and all the Outlaws' other trucks, cars and armored vehicles driven by her extended family straggling behind. She goes rolling up to the toll gate, where she pulls to a stop. Queenie will be too intent on what she is doing to see her beloved Prince hurl himself out of the truck and hit the ground in a windmilling confusion of arms and legs, fated to escape the reckoning.

She will not see him stagger away like a blind hermit, blundering to safety.

Queenie thinks: *Holy fuck, this is it. My big moment.*

She is not even sure what that is. All she knows is that she is sick of being shut out. The tollgate. That bitch! Flanked by the others she raises her gun. "Onward," she cries.

Which means that from her vantage point on the island, Courtney Ravenal punches in a command that activates the mines she has laid in the plaza at the toll gate and inadvertently blows Queenie's unfortunate family to oblivion.

For the first time in their lives, the Outlaws are on time for something. In this case, they are first.

And the nerve gas? Exploding, the cannisters release nothing but stale air. The damn things are duds. Once more the Outlaws have been betrayed by fate. At least it's for the last time.

❖

Troubled by this unexpected show of violence, the men withdraw. From a safe distance, they watch and wait.

❖

The inevitability of certain endings: K.'s friends A. and M. are both dead. And her mother? Speechless and still. Aware? But, ending? Not yet, not yet. Narrative provides alternatives.

❖

On the island, Chag is horrified by the explosion. She never intended this. She's too far away from the rubble to see stirring in the confusion of rubble and smoke. From where she stands it looks as though not a one of the Outlaws has survived. "My God!"

Courtney snaps, "Whatever. Look here. We are armed. We have supplies. We can hold them off."

The two women have come to a confrontation on the shore. The issue is the waiting delegation at the tollgate.

Courtney grins. "We can hold them off for the rest of our lives."

But Trini has limped into the circle, aided by Kitten Joe. "To what real purpose?"

Courtney wheels and with the butt of her Thompson gun attempts to silence Trini by smashing her in the face.

Kitten Joe is not swift enough to prevent all the damage but he manages to pull Trini aside before Courtney can hit her again, and Trini? Trini is—

Wait a minute. What's that sound? Trini is laughing!

Dredging up something she was told in grammar school,

the injured Sister Trinitas of the Little Sisters of the Apocalypse steps up to the infuriated Courtney. Instead of weeping and raging, she is renewed. She's like a girl, lighthearted and laughing. "It's supposed to be a sacrilege to hit a nun."

Courtney feints: she's ready to hit Trini again.

But Chag lunges, shouldering her out of the way. "What are you trying to do?"

"Can't you see it?" Courtney's blue eyes blaze in her pale face. Her black hair crackles like a thundercloud; she is wild. "We've gotten rid of them. Now we can be rid of them for good."

"If you mean the Outlaws, they're all dead."

"The Outlaws? Who cares about them?" Now it is out in the open. With a sweep of her arm Courtney will bring her army down on Chag and the Little Sisters of the Apocalypse. She speaks out of a stillness in which clocks stop.

"I mean the men."

For the moment, Chag stays Courtney's hand. She is after all the governor here and her word is still law.

"Men, women," Trini says thickly because her mouth is filling up with blood. "Can't you see that in the end we're all the same? What we are is, we're only *people.*"

She flashes on the lost vision: *the light, the light!*

Trini says, "In the end there's no real difference."

"Right." Courtney hits her again in spite of Chag and Kitten Joe. "Sure. That's why we are stuck here while these great big walking egos go out and have wars to make themselves feel good and then come back home and expect to find us with our legs spread. No difference. Sure."

In the eyes of God, Trini thinks, but cannot say because her mouth is torn and filled with blood.

Behind them the women of the island have begun to rally;

they are carrying weapons, most of them, although some are empty-handed. From this distance it is impossible to tell which of the women are allied with Courtney and which are not. Even the women aren't sure.

Then Courtney makes as if to bring down her army. As she does so Trini breaks free with an extraordinary final spurt of strength. "Men. Women." She tears the words out from somewhere deep. The vision is returning, spinning behind her eyes: women, men, everybody flying up like sparks, flickering aloft in the breathless split second before the final convergence. Then her eyes clear and for the first time ever Trini understands what she and the others are doing here.

They have been sent with the message. "Get this," she says. "*You're all the same.*"

It's not yet time for apocalypse, Trini realizes, not apocalypse nor revelation nor convergence, in spite of her hopes. What she saw in the instant she was pulled outside herself was a vision, not a roadmap or a guarantee. She sees it now.

It's as clear as if it is written: *There are no short cuts.*

Like the others she's only engaged in the continuing slow movement—perhaps upwards, but at its own pace. Tomorrow nothing much will be changed. They'll all just go on living. Like Steph and Nella, Trini understands that when it does end, life will not end easily and what's important now is to *survive*, and wait as gracefully as possible for some other hand to ring the curtain down.

It's like the next-to-last spring on the diving board, the hope that when the body takes to the air it will be magnificent.

In spite of what Trini had hoped for riding in, the Little Sisters of the Apocalypse are not on the island to preside over last things.

They are here for next-to-last things.

They are here to help each other go on.

"Men, women," she shouts to the grumbling women of Schell Isle, "Friends, enemies. It doesn't matter."

She tears free and hurls herself on the bike. The other sisters mount up and follow. Trini is racing now, ablaze with it. "People," she cries. "IT'S ALL THE SAME."

Next she says out of a stillness so great that they all turn to listen, "You have to help each other go forward."

Then she and the other fifteen roll out along the causeway, stationing themselves in pairs at intervals so that among them they protect the length of the road. Drawn up on their bikes, they are like sentinels or statues of mounted angels, marking or overseeing or is it defending or simply ensuring the return of the men.

❖

Not everybody is happy with this. Even the happy may not be happy forever, or even happy for long. This is the way it's going to be because this is the way it's always been. Happiness is fugitive, temporary at best. At least for now.

❖

Narrative has certain things in common with metaphysics. Perhaps one is an analog for the other: the consuming urge to discern or is it divine a scheme.

❖

The sisters assume their posts.

Two things happen.

Using a computer route Courtney isn't aware of, Chag disarms the electronic barrier. Flecks of debris, specks that used to be small animals and dead insects that have been suspended for years are freed; like ash, they come drifting down.

Courtney gives orders to her troops: *Attack!*

In the next second peaceful, bemused Jerome tackles her with surprising force and throws her down before she can do the job.

❖

Courtney tried to give the signal to attack. Everybody saw her do it; everybody heard her before this shaggy brute leveled her.

In spite of which, nobody's moved.

Nobody is moving.

Her women have the word. They know what she wants. Why have they not attacked?

The reasons are complex.

Right now in spite of the fact that their leader is valiantly struggling against the impassive Jerome, in spite of the fact that furious Courtney is still barking orders and raging, the women stand and wait.

❖

When the last of the Little Sisters of the Apocalypse has reached her station, Myrna lifts the toll gates.

The men begin their approach. Now across the causeway the first survivors come. Although they went out joyfully with guidons and marching bands, they are not triumphant now. They are not victors but survivors, because in spite of the declared victory the war was long and terrible and many were killed. Because they were committed to this thing, the men who were still living had to go on fighting even after doubt opened the door to despair.

Every institution develops an interest in its predictions and will act to protect them. D.P.M.

It's a matter of principle. The men declared this war. If they changed their minds and turned back they'd look like fools. Once committed, they had to fight to the bitter death.

Even for those who have managed to live through it the way home has been shatteringly hard. They are dirty, most of them; their drawn, bearded faces are rimed with sand caked in dried blood. Worn down by the exigencies of war, the men wear bits and scraps of uniforms from more than a dozen armies and what few flags they carry are too stained and tattered to be identified.

Some limp in on wrecked motorcycles while others approach by car while still others stagger on bandaged feet. Nobody runs or marches smartly: in some cases blood marks every footprint they leave in the road. They're reticent now, deferential and unarmed, as if the men think they'll be better received if they set aside weapons and unworthy gifts and approach their women empty-handed.

This is a sad procession, weary and after the events of the past few minutes, uncertain. *Does she still love me? Remember me?* Fearful of their reception, they move slowly. Have the magazines been filled with articles about how to treat a returning veteran, a lover who has been wounded in a hell of a way, a released POW? They used to be; these days, it's hard to know.

Troubled by the women's diffidence, they try: *We thought we were protecting you.* They're a pageant of hurt feelings. *What's the matter? We were doing it for you.*

❖

To Chag's astonishment and confusion, Toby comes first. She was ready to search for years, to go through hell and find him gravely altered and spend the rest of her life bringing him back. She was even prepared not to find him, to go through hell getting over it. She was not prepared for this.

Here he is.

❖

Even though she's screaming, the indeterminate number of women who make up Court's army stir but do not move. From the docks they watch their men file across the causeway, attempting the Return.

Here is a problem. Opening the front door for him, smoothing the pillow on his side of the bed, these women will forget certain things, but there are other things they can't forgive. Here are some of the things the women hold against their husbands, lovers:

—Times when he made it clear his concerns were more important than anything I did.

—Times he made me wait.

—Things he did to me.

—Things he said.

Here is the main reason the women may not want the men to come back, even the women who really do want them.

—IT'S GOING TO BE HARD.
They are looking to Chag.
They are waiting to see what she will do.

❖

It's going to be hard.

Chag looks at Toby. He is in bad shape. He's going to need more moral support than he can give back right now; he's going to take up a lot of room in her life. But God she is glad to see him.

Now he's grinning at her that same way and looking at her with those same eyes and in the crunch she finds herself throwing down the gauntlet. What is she doing, establishing the shibboleth? Drawing the line he has to cross? She does not say "Hello Toby," but of course he has not yet spoken.

Chag glares. *"And in the end the meaning's clear."* She's begging him to complete the password.

Toby doesn't say anything. He is looking at Chag so intently that his eyes cross. What is the matter with him? Can't he tell what's the matter with her? Idiot.

Doesn't he know how hard this is going to be?

There is the legend of the two halves of the egg, the children of the king kidnapped in their infancy, the unwitting lovers fated for each other, the twins separated at birth. All their lives ever since they have wandered, each of them with half of the crapula, uneven fragments that make no sense by themselves but when fused form a perfect whole. Picture two people running around the world, each with a piece of the puzzle; taken separately, the object in hand seems meaningless. The bearer knows it was created for a reason but does not know what.

Chag has presented Toby with one piece of the puzzle. She repeats: "*And in the end the meaning's clear.*"

Which Toby considers for a second. She can almost see his head snap back with the CLICK. Laughing, he starts: "*Don't ask what it is…*" Quits. Shouts. "*Chag!*"

Fuck doggerel. She laughs. "*You're here.*"

Then all their separate parts come together, warp into woof, ball into socket, yang liked with yin to make the circle complete; every protrusion clicks into the hollow it was created for—To what purpose? Another of life's mysteries. Everything fits together, but never the way you expect.

It is enough for now.

Chag and Toby can't know the future, what will be demanded of them or even what's intended, but here they are. Remember, it is Toby who asks to come back into her life and Chag who permits this—enabling the Return. Understand, while he was out being diminished, she was waiting. Getting strong. No. Even stronger.

❖

This is not the end. It isn't even the ending of the story. Half-buried in debris on the far side of the causeway, Queenie groans and tries to sit up. As she does so she is stirred by the pressure of a thousand furry bodies; half-blinded by a paste of dirt and blood, she won't know what's happening, only that she's being nudged and licked and massaged and finally carried along to a place where, surrounded by the cats that have left Jerome and, under cover of the Return swarmed over the lakebed to rescue and reinforce her, she can regroup and consider her next move.

And Courtney? Writhing in Jerome's determined grasp, Courtney numbers the affronts and begins to plot the revolution, while on the island women everywhere assess their position. He is at their gates and once they let him inside there's no telling what he'll do. He loves her. He does! OK, she's spent too much time imagining the Return to thwart this reunion. Will she be sorry or glad? She can't know. There is only one thing she does know, and it's this.

Nothing is forever.

❖

Honey, I'm back.

Don't you love me, honey?

I love you. I do!

At last he says what she's been waiting to hear. *You know I'll do anything for you.*

"Anything I say?"

He's exhausted; he's hungry, he wants her *so much.* Truthful or not, he says, "Anything."

❖

The women's army drops its weapons and holds out its arms. He's back, but on her terms. She's won this without firing a shot.

❖

This isn't the end either. Art doesn't provide endings, only convenient places to stop. The possibility of creating order. And life? It's still fraught with peril. And every day—no matter how terrible—we have to get up in the morning and keep going.

❖

Time breaks even the fiercest concentration. Leaves fall. Ponds freeze. Your body tells you it's time to come back from wherever you thought you were going. You stop to refuel but you know the last voyage out has brought you one step closer to whatever you thought you were approaching. Narrative offers the possibility for closure. Narrative can be neat.

Life is not, but in either case there is inevitability.

Lillian Hyde Craig. April 28, 1905-December 24, 1992.

❖

Lights go on in the kitchens and bedrooms of the women's houses. He's home, perhaps for good. It's already hard. Her kindness is matched by her tolerance.

When the world ends, the last person left standing will be a woman.

1988-1994

176